"Do you know how to shoot a gun?" he asked.

"Doesn't matter," he added quickly as he pulled the gun from behind him and handed it to her through the window. "It's ready to go. All you have to do is pull the trigger. Aim for the largest part of a person." He saw her cringe. "You can do this."

She nodded, a determined look settling on her features.

He gave her a smile, then pulled off his glove and reached through the broken window to touch her face with his fingertips. She closed her eyes, leaning into his warm palm. Tears beaded her lashes when he pulled his hand away.

CHRISTMAS AT CARDWELL RANCH

—

B.J. DANIELS

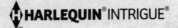
HARLEQUIN® INTRIGUE®

Recycling programs
for this product may
not exist in your area.

In memory of Rita Ness, who will always
be remembered as the bright ray of sunshine
she was. She is dearly missed.

ISBN-13: 978-0-373-69722-9

CHRISTMAS AT CARDWELL RANCH

Copyright © 2013 by Barbara Heinlein

Printed in U.S.A.

ABOUT THE AUTHOR

USA TODAY bestselling author B.J. Daniels wrote her first book after a career as an award-winning newspaper journalist and author of thirty-seven published short stories. That first book, *Odd Man Out,* received a four-and-a-half-star review from *RT Book Reviews* and went on to be nominated for Best Intrigue that year. Since then, she has won numerous awards, including a career achievement award for romantic suspense and many nominations and awards for best book.

Daniels lives in Montana with her husband, Parker, and two springer spaniels, Spot and Jem. When she isn't writing, she snowboards, camps, boats and plays tennis. Daniels is a member of Mystery Writers of America, Sisters in Crime, International Thriller Writers, Kiss of Death and Romance Writers of America.

To contact her, write to B.J. Daniels, P.O. Box 1173, Malta, MT 59538, or email her at bjdaniels@mtintouch.net. Check out her website, www.bjdaniels.com.

Books by B.J. Daniels

CAST OF CHARACTERS

Tanner "Tag" Cardwell—He'd come to Montana to have Christmas with his father and cousin Dana—until he found himself embroiled in a murder mystery too close to home.

Lily McCabe—The mathematician and college professor always thought she wanted a safe, quiet life with a man who loved math as much as she did. Then she met Tag.

Gerald Humphrey—Six months ago he'd stood his fiancée up at the altar. Now he was back. But what did he really want?

James "Ace" McCabe—The good-looking owner of The Canyon bar loved the night life at Big Sky—and having his sister Lily work with him over the holidays.

Mia Duncan—The Canyon bar cocktail waitress had the kind of secret that could get a woman killed.

Harlan Cardwell—He was a man who loved nothing more than beer and playing his guitar. Or was he?

Teresa Evans—The waitress at The Canyon bar thought she had problems—until she decided to walk home that snowy night just before Christmas.

Hud Cardwell—The marshal had his hands full with a murderer on the loose and a target on his back.

Chapter One

Huge snowflakes drifted down out of a midnight-blue winter sky. Tanner "Tag" Cardwell stopped to turn his face up to the falling snow. It had been so long since he'd been anywhere that it snowed like this.

Christmas lights twinkled in all the windows of the businesses of Big Sky's Meadow Village, and he could hear "White Christmas" playing in one of the ski shops.

But it was a different kind of music that called to him tonight as he walked through the snow to the Canyon Bar.

Shoving open the door, he felt a wave of warmth hit him, along with the smell of beer and the familiar sound of country music.

He smiled as the band broke into an old country-and-western song, one he'd learned at his father's knee. Tag let the door close behind him on the winter night and shook snow from his new ski jacket as he looked around. He'd had to buy the coat because for the past twenty-one years, he'd been living down South.

Friday night just days from Christmas in Big Sky, Montana, the bar was packed with a mix of locals, skiers, snowmobilers and cowboys. There'd be a fight for sure before the night was over. He planned to be long gone before then, though.

His gaze returned to the raised platform where the band, Canyon Cowboys, was playing. He played a little guitar himself, but he'd never been as good as his father, he thought as he watched Harlan Cardwell pick and strum to the music. His uncle, Angus Cardwell, was no slouch, either.

Tag had always loved listening to them play together when he was a kid. Music was in their blood. That and bars. As a kid, he'd fallen asleep many weekend nights in a bar in this canyon listening to his father play guitar. It was one of the reasons his mother had gathered up her five sons, divorced Harlan and taken her brood off to Texas to be raised in the Lone Star State.

Tag and his brothers had been angry with their dad for not fighting for them. As they'd gotten older, they'd realized their mother had done them a favor. Harlan knew nothing about raising kids. He was an easygoing cowboy who only came alive when you handed him a guitar—or a beer.

Still, as Tag watched his father launch into another song, he realized how much he'd missed him—and Montana. Had Harlan missed him, as well? Doubtful, Tag thought, remembering the reception he'd gotten when he'd knocked at his father's cabin door this morning.

"Tag?"

"Surprise."

"What are you doing here?" his father had asked, moving a little to block his view of the interior of the cabin.

"It's Christmas. I wanted to spend it with you."

Harlan couldn't have looked any more shocked by that—or upset.

Tag realized that surprising his father had been a mistake. "If this is a bad time…"

His father quickly shook his head, still blocking the door, though. "No, it's just that…well, you know, the cabin is a mess. If you give me a little while…"

Tag peered past him and lowered his voice. "If you have someone staying here—"

"No, no, it's nothing like that."

But behind his father, Tag had spotted a leather jacket, female size, on the arm of the couch. "No problem. I thought I'd go see my cousin Dana. I'll come back later. Actually, if you want, I could get a motel—"

"No. Stay here. Bring your stuff back later. I'll have the spare room made up for you. Your uncle and I are playing tonight at the Canyon."

"Great. I'll stop by. I haven't heard you play in a long time. It'll be nice."

Tag had left, but he was still curious about his father's female visitor. He knew nothing about his father's life. Harlan could have a girlfriend. It wasn't that unusual for a good-looking man in his fifties.

Tag tried not to let Harlan's reaction to him showing up unexpectedly bother him. Determined to enjoy the holiday here, he had made plans tomorrow to go Christmas tree hunting with his Montana cousin Dana Cardwell. He'd missed his cousins and had fond memories of winter in Montana, sledding, skiing, ice-skating, starting snowball fights and cutting their own Christmas trees. He looked forward to seeing his cousins Jordan and Stacy, as well. Clay was still in California helping make movies last he'd heard, but Dana had said he was flying in Christmas Eve.

Tag planned to do all the things he had done as a boy this Christmas. Not that he could ever bring back those family holidays he remembered. For starters, his four brothers were all still in Texas. The five of them had started a barbecue joint, which had grown into a chain called Texas Boys Barbecue.

He would miss his brothers and mother this Christmas, but he was glad to have this time with his cousins and his dad. As the band wound up one song and quickly broke into another, he finished his beer. He'd see his father back at the cabin. Earlier, he'd returned to find the woman's leather jacket he'd seen on the couch long gone.

Harlan had been getting ready for his gig tonight, so they hadn't had much time to visit. But the spare room had been made up, so Tag had settled in. He hoped to spend some time with his father, though. Maybe tomorrow after he came back from Christmas tree hunting.

As he started to turn to leave, a blonde smelling of alcohol stumbled into him. Tag caught her as she clung to his ski jacket for support. She was dressed in jeans and a T-shirt. Not one of the skiers or snowmobilers who were duded out in the latest high-tech, cold-weather gear.

"Sorry," she said, slurring her speech.

"Are you all right?" he asked as she clung to his jacket for a moment before gathering her feet under her.

"Fine." She didn't look fine at all. Clearly, she'd had way too much to drink. "You look like him."

Tag laughed. Clearly, the woman also didn't know what she was saying.

She lurched away from him and out the back door.

He couldn't believe with it snowing so hard that she'd gone outside without a coat. Hesitating only a moment, he went out after her. He was afraid she might be planning to drive herself home. Or that she had been hurrying outside because she was going to be sick. He didn't want her passing out in a snowdrift and dying of hypothermia.

Montana was nothing like where he lived in Texas. Winter in Montana could be dangerous. With this winter storm, the temperatures had dropped. There were already a couple of feet of snow out the back door of the bar before this latest snowfall. He could see that a good six inches of new snow had fallen since he'd arrived in town.

He spotted the woman's tracks in the snow just outside the door. As he stepped out to look for her, he saw her through the falling snow. A man wearing a cowboy hat was helping her into his pickup. She appeared to be arguing with him as he poured her into the passenger seat and slammed the door. The man glanced in Tag's direction for a moment before he climbed behind the wheel and the two drove off.

"Where did she go?"

He turned to find a slim brunette behind him. "Where did who go?"

"Mia." At his blank expression, she added, "The blonde woman wearing a T-shirt like the one I have on."

He glanced at her T-shirt and doubted any woman could wear it quite the way this one did. The letters THE CANYON were printed across her full breasts with the word *bar* in smaller print beneath it. He realized belatedly that the woman who'd bumped into him had been wearing the same T-shirt—like the other servers here in the bar.

"I *did* see her," he said. "She stumbled into me, then went rushing out this door."

"Unbelievable," the brunette said with a shake of her head. Her hair was chin length, thick and dark. It framed a face that could only be described as adorable. "She didn't finish her shift again tonight."

"She wasn't in any shape to continue her shift," he said. "She could barely stand up she was so drunk."

For the first time, the brunette met his gaze. "Mia might have had one drink because a customer insisted, but there is no way she was drunk. I saw her ten minutes ago and she was fine."

He shrugged. "I saw her two minutes ago and she was falling-down drunk. She didn't even bother with her coat."

"And you let her leave like that?"

"Apparently her boyfriend or husband was waiting for her. The cowboy poured her into the passenger seat of his pickup and they left."

"She doesn't *have* a boyfriend or a husband."

"Well, she left with some man wearing a Western hat. That's all I can tell you." He remembered that the blonde had been arguing with the man and felt a sliver of unease embed itself under his skin. Still, he told himself, he'd had the distinct feeling that she'd known the man. Nor had the cowboy acted odd when he'd looked in Tag's direction before leaving.

"Lily!" the male bartender called. The brunette gave another disgusted shake of her head, this one directed at Tag, before she took off back into the bar.

He watched her, enjoying the angry swing of her hips. Then he headed for his father's cabin, tired after flying all the way from Texas today. But he couldn't help thinking of the brunette and smiling to himself. He'd always been a sucker for a woman with an attitude.

LILY MCCABE CLOSED the front door of the Canyon Bar behind the last customer, locked it and leaned against the solid wood for a moment. What a night.

"Nice job," Ace said as he began cleaning behind the bar. "Where the devil did Mia take off to?"

Lily shook her head. It was the second night in a row that Mia had disappeared. What made it odd was that she'd been so reliable for the three weeks she'd been employed at the Canyon. It was hard to get good help. Mia Duncan was one of the good ones.

"It's weird," Lily said as she grabbed a tray to clear off the tables. In the far back, the other two servers were already at work doing the same thing. "The man who saw her take off out the back door? He claimed she was *drunk*."

James "Ace" McCabe stopped what he was doing to stare at her. "Mia, drunk?"

Lily shrugged as she thought of the dark-haired cowboy with the Texas accent. Men like him were too good-looking to start with. Add a Southern drawl… "That's what he said. I believe his exact words were 'falling-down drunk,'" she mimicked in his Texas accent. "Doesn't sound like Mia, does it? Plus, I talked to her not ten minutes before. She was fine. He must have been mistaken."

Admittedly, she knew Mia hardly at all. The young woman wasn't from Big Sky. But then most people in the Gallatin Canyon right now weren't locals. Ski season brought in people from all over the world. Mia had shown up one day looking for a job. One of the servers had just quit and another had broken her leg skiing, so James had hired Mia on the spot. That was over three weeks ago. Mia had been great. Until last night when she'd left before her shift was over—and again tonight.

"Well, tonight was a real zoo," Reggie Olson said as she brought in a tray full of dirty glasses from a table in the back. "The closer it gets to the holidays, the crazier it gets."

Lily couldn't have agreed more. She couldn't wait for Christmas and New Year's to be over so she could get back to her real life.

"Did Mia say anything to either of you?" she asked.

Reggie shook her head.

Teresa Evans didn't seem to hear.

"Teresa," Lily called to the back of the bar. "Did Mia say anything to you tonight before she left?"

Teresa glanced up in surprise at the sound of her name, her mind clearly elsewhere. "Sorry?"

"Someone's tired," Ace said with a laugh.

"More likely she's thinking about her boyfriend waiting for her outside in his pickup," Reggie joked.

Teresa looked flustered. "I guess I *am* tired," she said. "Mia?" She shook her head. "She didn't say anything to me."

That, too, was odd since Teresa was as close to a friend as Mia had made in the weeks she'd worked at the bar. Lily noticed how distracted the server was and wanted to ask her if everything was all right. But her brother was their boss, not she. His approach during her short-term employment here was not to get involved in his employees' dramas. Probably wise since once the holiday was over, she would be going back to what she considered her "real" life.

"Maybe you should give Mia a call," Lily suggested.

Her brother gave her one of his patient smiles, looked up Mia's number and dialed it. "She's not home," he said after he listened for a few moments. "And I don't have a cell phone number for her."

"If she left with some cowboy, she must have a boyfriend we haven't heard about," Reggie said. "He's probably the reason she was drinking, too," she added with a laugh. "Men. Can't live with them. Can't shoot them."

Ace laughed. "Reggie's right. Go ahead and go on home, sis," he said when she brought up a tray of dirty glasses. "The three of us can finish up here. And thanks again for helping out."

She'd agreed to help her brother over Christmas and New Year's, and had done so for the past few. Since it was just the two of them, their parents gone, it was as close as they got to a family holiday together. The bar was her brother's only source of income, and with this being his busiest time of the year, he had to have all the help he could get.

Ace had learned a long time ago that if he didn't work his own place, he lost money. With Lily helping, he didn't have to hire another server. She didn't need the money since her "day" job paid very well and working at the Canyon gave her a chance to spend time with the brother she adored.

"I *am* going to call it a night," Lily said, dumping her tips into the communal tip jar at the bar. Her Big Sky home was a house she'd purchased back up the mountain tucked in the pines about five miles from the bar—and civilization. The house had been an investment. Not that she could have stayed with her brother since he lived in the very small apartment over the bar. Christmas would be spent at her house, as it was every year.

When she'd bought the house, she'd thought Ace would move in since her real home and work was forty miles away in Bozeman. But her brother had only laughed and said he was much happier living over the bar in the apartment.

Lily loved the house because of its isolation at the end of a road with no close neighbors—the exact reason

Ace would have hated living there. Her brother loved to be around people. He liked the noise and commotion that came with owning a bar in Big Sky, Montana.

But as much as she yearned to go to her quiet house, she couldn't yet. She wanted to make sure Mia made it home all right. Mia lived in an expensive condo her parents owned partway up the mountain toward Big Sky Resort.

Lily noticed Mia's down ski jacket where she'd hung it before her shift, her worry increasing when under it she found Mia's purse hanging from its shoulder strap. She left both there, thinking Mia might return to retrieve them. As she went out the back door of the bar, she saw that it was still snowing. She glanced toward Lone Mountain, disappointed the falling snow obliterated everything. She loved seeing the mountain peak glistening white against the dark winter sky. It really was a magnificent sight.

Thinking of the skiers who would be delirious tomorrow with all this fresh powder, she had to smile. She understood why her brother loved living here. The Gallatin Canyon was a magical place—especially at Christmas.

The Gallatin River, which cut through the steep, granite bluffs in a breathtaking hundred-mile ribbon of river and winding highway, ran crystal clear under a thick blanket of ice. Snow covered the mountains and weighted down the pine boughs, making the entire place a winter wonderland.

Before the ski resort, the canyon had been mostly cattle and dude ranches, a few summer cabins and even fewer homes. Now luxury houses had sprouted up all around the resort. Fortunately some of the original cabins still remained and the majority of the canyon was national forest, so it would always remain undeveloped.

The "canyon" was still its own little community made up of permanent residents as well as those who only showed up for a week or two in the summer and a few weeks around Christmas and New Year's for the ski season.

Outside, her breath expelled in cold white puffs. She hugged herself as she looked through the driving snow and saw Mia's car. Mia was always so protective of her car. It seemed strange that she would leave it. But if she really had been drunk… Maybe she was planning to come back.

Who had she left with, though? Some cowboy, the Texan had said. That, too, didn't sound like Mia, let alone that the cowboy had "poured her into the passenger seat."

Everything about this felt wrong.

Unable to shake off the bad feeling that had settled over her, Lily headed for her SUV. The drive up to Mia's condo didn't take long in the wee hours of the morning after the bars had closed. There was no traffic and few tracks in the fresh snow that now blanketed the narrow paved road. Her windshield wipers clacked noisily trying to keep up with the falling snow, and yet visibility in her headlights was still only a matter of yards.

Lily was used to driving in winter conditions, having been born and raised in Montana, but just the thought of accidentally sliding off the road on such a night gave her a chill. Why hadn't she told her brother where she was going?

She'd heard tomorrow was supposed to clear, the storm moving on. With a full moon tomorrow night, maybe she would go cross-country skiing. She loved skiing at night in the moonlight. It was so peaceful and quiet.

Through the falling snow, she got glimpses of Christmas lights twinkling on the houses she passed. She'd already done all her Christmas shopping, but she was sure her brother would be waiting until the last minute. They were so different. She was just thankful they were close in spite of their differences, even though Ace was always trying to get her to loosen up. He saw her orderly life as boring.

"You need to have some fun, sis," he'd said recently when he'd given her a ski pass and the ultimatum that she was to use it on her day off. "It will do you good."

She didn't need Ace to tell her what else he thought would do her good. She'd forbidden him to even mention her former fiancé Gerald's name. Not that it often stopped him.

Distracted with her thoughts, she saw that she'd reached her destination. But as she pulled up in front of Mia's condo, her earlier bad feeling turned to dread.

Mia's front door stood open. A drift of freshly fallen snow had formed just inside the door.

Chapter Two

The hair stood up on the back of Lily's neck as she got out of her SUV and walked toward the gaping front door.

"Mia?" she called as she carefully peered in. She could hear music playing inside the condo. Mia's unit was on the end, and it appeared that whoever was staying in the adjacent one wasn't home.

Lily touched the door. It creaked the rest of the way open. From the doorway, she had a view of the stairs. One set went up, the other down.

"Mia?" she called over the music. No answer as she carefully stepped in.

She'd only gone a few steps up the stairs when she saw what appeared to be a fist-size ball of cotton roll across the floor on the breeze coming in the open door behind her.

One more step and she saw dozens of white balls of cotton. Her heart began to pound. Another step and she saw what was left of the living room sofa cushions.

The condo looked as if it had been hit by a storm that had wreaked havoc on the room. The sofa cushions had been shredded, the stuffing now moving haphazardly around the room. Lamps lay broken in pieces of jagged glass shards on the wooden floor. A chair had been turned over, the bottom ripped out. Nothing in the room looked as if it had weathered the storm that had blown through here.

Who would do such a thing? Why would they? Lily fumbled out her cell phone as she backed down the stairs, her heart hammering against her rib cage. What if whoever had done this was still in the condo?

"I need to report a break-in," she said the moment she reached her SUV and was safely inside. She kept her eyes on the open doorway. When the dispatcher at the local marshal's office answered, she hurriedly gave her name and the address.

"Is the intruder still there?"

"I don't know. I only went just inside the door."

"Where are you now?"

"I'm outside. I don't know where the owner of the condo is. I'm worried about her."

"Can you wait in a warm place?"

"Yes. I'm in my vehicle and watching the condo."

"Please stay there until law enforcement arrives."

MARSHAL HUD SAVAGE was on duty when the call came in. He'd just been up on the mountain on a disturbance call. All day he'd felt as if he were moving in a fog. A cop friend of his from the academy had been killed two nights ago. He was still in shock.

Paul Brown's death, on top of what had happened to Hud's family last spring, had left him shaken. In April, he'd let a dangerous woman come into his home. Hud's wife and children had almost been killed.

He was a *marshal*. He should have seen what was right in front of his eyes. He would never forgive himself. Worse, the incident really had him questioning if he had the instincts anymore for this job.

When he'd heard that his friend Paul had been murdered just forty miles away in Bozeman, he'd been ready to throw in the towel.

"I'm running scared," he'd told his wife, Dana.

She'd hugged him and tried to persuade him that none of what had happened to their family was his fault. "I was the one who was so excited to have a cousin I'd never met come stay with us. You saw that I was happy and ignored things you wouldn't have under any other circumstances."

"I'm a *marshal,* Dana. There is no excuse for what happened last April. None."

Now as he turned into the condo subdivision in the pines, he tried to push everything but this latest call out of his mind. More and more, though, he wasn't sure he deserved to be wearing this star.

As he pulled up, a young brunette got out of her SUV and stood hugging herself against the cold snowy night. A break-in this time of year was unusual. Normally this sort of thing happened during off-season when there were fewer people around.

"Are you the one who made the call?" he asked as he got out of his patrol pickup.

She introduced herself as Lily McCabe.

"Ace's sister," he said with a nod.

"Sometimes I forget how small a community Big Sky is," she said, not looking in the least bit happy about the prospect that everyone knew her business.

Gossip traveled fast in the canyon. Hud had heard something about Ace's sister being left at the altar. He couldn't imagine any sane man leaving this woman.

"Wait in your vehicle while I take a look inside," he told her. But as he headed for the open front door, he saw that she was still standing outside as if too nervous to sit and wait.

At the door, he pulled his weapon and stepped in, even though he doubted the burglar was still inside. The condo had been ransacked in a way that surprised him. This was no normal break-in. Nor was it a simple case of vandalism. Whoever had done this was looking for something and was determined to destroy everything in his path if he didn't find it.

He moved carefully through the upper floor, then the lower one, before he returned to the woman waiting outside.

"Is she…"

He shook his head. "No sign of anyone. I've called for backup. Until they get here, can we talk in your vehicle?"

She nodded and climbed behind the wheel. She'd left the SUV running, so it was warm inside. He couldn't help noticing how neat and clean the interior was as he pulled out his notebook. "Whose condo is it?"

"I don't know their name. Mia told me that her parents own it. She is the one who's been staying here."

"Mia?"

"Mia Duncan. She went to work for my brother at the Canyon three weeks ago. I'm here helping out over the holidays, as you apparently know."

He nodded. He'd heard Ace's sister had bought a house about four years ago up the mountain—about the same time her brother had opened the Canyon Bar.

"Were you meeting Mia here after work?"

Lily shook her head. "She left before her shift was over. I was worried about her, so I decided to drive up and check on her."

"Did she say why she left?"

"No. That's just it. She didn't say anything. One of our patrons saw her leave with a man. The patron said he thought she'd been drinking."

He sensed that she didn't see how any of this helped and hated talking about Mia behind her back. "Could the man she left with have been a boyfriend?"

"She'd said she wasn't seeing anyone, but I can't swear to it."

"Did this patron describe the man he saw her leave with?"

"Just that he was wearing a cowboy hat and driving a pickup."

"That doesn't narrow it down much. What is this patron's name?"

She shook her head. "I've never seen him before. I'm sorry that I can't offer much in the way of details. He had a Southern accent, if that helps."

"You're doing fine. Did you see anyone leaving as you drove into the condo complex tonight?"

"No. But as soon as I pulled up here, I saw that her door was partially open. I only went a few steps inside before I called you."

He'd seen her footprints in the snow. Unfortunately, the footprints of the intruder had been covered by fresh snow. Someone who knew Mia's hours at the bar and knew she wouldn't be coming home until the bar closed? But she left early. So where was she?

Hud wrote down Lily's cell phone number and closed his notebook as another patrol rig drove up. "I'll call if I have any more questions."

"I don't know Mia well, but I'm worried about her. This is the second night she's left in the middle of her shift without telling anyone. Before that she was our most reliable employee."

He nodded. If it wasn't for the ransacked condo, he would have just figured the woman had met some man and fallen hard. People in love often became less reliable employees.

Hud assured Lily he'd let her know when he heard something. But he could tell nothing he might say would relieve her worry. After seeing the inside of the condo, he shared her concern.

With her shift finally over, Teresa Evans opened the back door of the bar and looked out at the falling snow. She had mixed feelings about seeing her boyfriend after the fight they'd had earlier before she'd left for work.

But she didn't have to worry about it. The main parking lot was empty. No Ethan sitting out here in his old pickup, the engine running, the wipers trying to keep up with the falling snow. No Ethan at all.

The only vehicles were Reggie's SUV and Ace's old Jeep. Both were covered in snow.

"Do you need a ride?" Reggie asked behind her, making her jump. The other server stopped to frown at her. "Are you all right?"

"I'm fine," she said a little too sharply.

Reggie raised an eyebrow.

"Didn't Lily say Mia left with someone else earlier?" Teresa asked. "Her car's gone."

Reggie glanced to the spot where Mia had parked earlier. Teresa followed her gaze. There was a rectangular spot in the snow where the car had been.

"I guess she must have come back for it," Reggie said with a shrug. "I hope she wasn't as drunk as that customer thought she was. Bad night to be driving as it is."

"Yeah," Teresa agreed. "Or to be working."

took hold of her arm and gently squeezed

it through Teresa's coat. "Hey, accidents happen. Ace knows that."

It took her a moment to realize that Reggie was referring to the tray of glasses she'd dropped earlier in the evening when she was clearing one of the tables. "Clumsy," she said to cover the truth. "I think I'm coming down with something."

"Is everything okay with Ethan?" Reggie asked, lowering her voice, as they stood under the shelter of the small landing just outside the bar. Reggie didn't look at her when she asked it. Instead, she pretended more interest in digging her keys out of her purse.

Teresa stared through the falling snow, trying to conjure Ethan and his old pickup. "We're good." That wasn't exactly true, but it was too cold to get into it out here in the wee hours of the morning. "I appreciate you asking, though."

"Hey, we're friends. You sure you don't want a ride?" Reggie said, looking around as she found her keys in the bottom of her shoulder bag. "I don't see Ethan."

"He'll be along soon. He probably just fell asleep. I'll give him a call. If worse comes to worst, I'll walk. It's not that far."

Reggie looked skeptical. "You'd be soaked to the skin if you walked in this." But she let it drop, no doubt sensing that whatever was going on with Teresa, it wasn't something she wanted to talk about. "Well, then, I'll see you tomorrow. I just hope it won't be as crazy as it was tonight." With that, Reggie stepped off the covered landing and headed for her car.

Teresa found herself wondering when Mia had come back for her vehicle as she watched Reggie clean the snow from her car and finally drive away. She couldn't shake the memory of what Mia had said to her earlier.

Several cars went by, disappearing quickly into the falling snow. Still no sign of Ethan. Reaching into her pocket, she told herself he had probably fallen asleep and forgotten to set the alarm. Her pocket was empty. She tried the other one. Empty. With a groan, she remembered leaving her cell phone on the breakfast bar earlier. She'd been in such a rush to get out of the apartment and away from Ethan, she'd forgotten it.

Ethan wasn't coming. Had she really expected him to come after the fight they'd had? She considered going back inside the bar to wait, but she didn't want Ace to know Ethan had stood her up. As soon as Reggie's taillights disappeared in the snowstorm, Teresa started the walk home.

The fight earlier had been another of those stupid ones.

"I need to know you want to marry me and have this baby," he'd said while she was getting ready for work.

"Stop pressuring me." Ever since she'd told him she was pregnant, he'd been so protective that sometimes she couldn't breathe. He was determined they had to get married and settle down. His idea of settling down was moving closer to his parents, who lived down in Billings.

"I don't think your new friend Mia is good for you. I saw her talking to some guy the other day. I've seen him before. He's bad news."

Teresa stifled a groan.

"I don't want you getting involved in some drug deal, or worse."

She had turned to face him, unable to hide her growing impatience. Ethan had been like this ever since he'd gone to the law enforcement academy and was now working for the Montana Highway Patrol.

"I'm sure Mia isn't involved in any kind of drug deal."

"Your friend might not realize what she's getting herself into with a man like that."

It made her angry to hear him talk this way. "Mia's a big girl," she'd snapped. "She can take care of herself." When Ethan looked skeptical, she'd added, "Mia carries a gun." Instantly, she'd wished she hadn't added that part.

"She *what?*" he'd demanded.

"It's just a small one. She wears it strapped on her ankle."

Ethan had sworn and begun to pace. "You're hanging out with a woman who carries a concealed weapon? Does she even have a permit to carry it?"

"Damn it, Ethan. Stop acting like a narc."

He had stopped dead in his tracks. *"What?"*

"It's just that you used to be fun. Now you're such a..."

He had waited for her to finish.

"Cop."

Without another word, he'd grabbed his coat and left.

Still, she couldn't imagine him not picking her up. He was too concerned about her and the baby. Something must have come up with his job, she thought now as she walked through the deep snow toward the apartment they shared.

Ethan had been her high school sweetheart. She smiled to herself now as she thought of how they'd been back then. He had been adventurous, up for anything. His friends said he was crazy fun.

But a couple of years ago, he'd almost gotten into some serious trouble with some ex-friends of his. The incident had apparently scared him straight. He was no longer crazy fun. Far from it.

Teresa wasn't sure she wanted to be married to a cop. She wasn't sure she wanted to be married to Ethan. She wasn't even sure she wanted to be pregnant.

Shoving those thoughts away, she found herself worrying about Mia as she ducked her head against the thick falling snow. Tonight she'd seen Mia get into some kind of argument with a man who'd come into the bar alone. The conversation had looked personal—and definitely heated. At one point the man had grabbed Mia's arm. In the skirmish, the man ended up spilling his drink on her.

Teresa had quickly stepped in.

"Back off. I have it under control," Mia had snapped, wiping at her alcohol-soaked jeans.

Teresa might have argued differently, but the man had raised his head and looked right at her before getting up and leaving.

Mia had apologized a while later when they'd both gone up to the bar to get their drink orders. "I just didn't want you getting involved." Mia's gaze had met hers, worry in her eyes. "I might have already involved you too much. I'm sorry."

She'd been startled by her words. Even more startled when Mia had gone to the room where they kept their coats. Teresa saw Mia take something out of Teresa's ski jacket pocket and stuff it into her jeans pocket.

Teresa had confronted her, only to have Mia pull away. She'd stood helplessly as Mia grabbed her tray of drinks and headed off through the crowd toward one of the large tables at the back of the bar.

Not long after that Mia had seemed unsteady on her feet.

As Teresa had gone back over to the empty table where the man had been sitting, to clear his table, she spotted the hypodermic needle lying under his chair. Her heart had begun to pound. Was Ethan right? Was the argument over drugs?

It still gave her chills to remember the look on the man's face when he'd glanced up at her. Not long after that, she'd seen Mia stagger into some man before leaving through the back door. Mia had definitely appeared drugged. Had she left with the man?

She felt a chill now as she slogged through the deep snow, glad she wasn't that far from home. She'd left behind the cluster of buildings that made up the center of Meadow Village. Now there was nothing but snowy darkness. Pines, their branches heavy with snow, stood like sentinels at the edge of the mountain to her right. To her left, the golf course was an empty field of deep snow.

The storm hadn't let up for hours. She kept her head down against the falling snow, but it still clung to her face and eyelashes. With each step, she regretted not going back into the bar and calling Ethan. Sometimes she was her own worst enemy.

At the sound of a car approaching, she moved to the edge of the road. Probably Ethan, she thought. Was it possible he'd simply fallen asleep and on awakening, realized he hadn't picked her up?

She felt headlights wash over her. Chilled to the bone, she could feel the deep wet snow soaking into her jeans up to her knees. She was angry with him, but right now she didn't feel like fighting. Worse, she didn't want her own foolish stubbornness to make her end up walking the rest of the way home just to spite Ethan or try to make him feel guilty.

Once they got back to the apartment, she would take a nice hot shower. Maybe have a beer with him. Or a soda, she thought, remembering that she was pregnant. She might even be up for making love. Anything to take the edge off and forget for just a while that her life was a mess and had been as far back as she could remember.

Teresa shielded her eyes from the blizzard and the bright headlights as the vehicle caught up to her. A thought struck her in that instant. The engine sound was wrong. She knew it wasn't Ethan in his old pickup even before she saw the large black SUV slow to a stop next to her.

It was one of those expensive big rigs like ones she saw all over Big Sky. The windows were dark as well as the paint. She was trying to see inside, to see if she knew the driver, when the back door was suddenly flung open.

The man who jumped out was large and bundled up in a bulky coat. Her heart was already racing by the time he grabbed her. She tried to scream, but he clamped a gloved hand over her mouth and dragged her toward the large SUV. She fought, but he was too strong for her. Still, she got in a few good kicks and punches before he forced a smelly cloth over her mouth and nose, and everything went black.

Chapter Three

Hud got the call just after daylight the next morning. He'd been up all night with the break-in. He needed sleep and food badly, and was on his way home, hoping for both when the call came in.

"My fiancée didn't come home last night."

"Who am I speaking with?" he asked. The man sounded more than a little upset.

"Ethan Cross."

Hud knew Ethan, knew his record. A wild, good-looking kid who'd gotten into trouble a lot before going to the academy and becoming a highway patrol officer.

"Your fiancée is Teresa Evans?" he asked to clarify. Ethan had been with Teresa since high school. That was the nice thing about a small community. Hud knew the players, at least the local ones.

"She works at the Canyon. I was supposed to pick her up after closing, but I got called out on an accident down by Fir Ridge. With the roads like they were, I didn't get back in time. When I realized she wasn't home, I went looking for her. This isn't like her."

Hud took a guess. "Did the two of you have a fight earlier yesterday?" It was an old story, one he'd heard many times.

"Not really a fight exactly. Still, she wouldn't not come home."

"She probably just stayed at a friend's place to let things cool down. Have you checked with any of her friends?"

"There's only one she's been tight with recently. I tried Mia's number, but she doesn't answer."

"Mia Duncan?" Hud asked, and felt his pulse quicken when Ethan said yes. "Have you tried Teresa's cell phone?"

"She forgot to take it when she left for work. I found it when I called her number looking for her."

"Let's give her a few hours and see if she doesn't turn up," Hud said, hoping he didn't have two missing women, since Mia Duncan hadn't turned up yet, either.

TAG COULDN'T BELIEVE how much he'd missed this. As he trod through the knee-high snow on the mountain the next morning swinging the ax, he breathed in the frosty air and the sweet fresh smell of pine.

"How about that one?" Dana called from below him on the mountainside. They had climbed up the mountain behind his cousin's ranch house Christmas tree hunting. Now she motioned at one to his far right.

He waded through the new-fallen snow to check the tree, shook off the branches, then called back, "Too flat on the back. I'm going up higher on the mountain."

"There's an old logging road up there," she called from down below. "I'll meet you where it comes out. If you find a tree, give a holler. Meanwhile, I'll keep looking down here." She sounded as if she was enjoying this as much as he was, but then Dana had always loved the great outdoors.

He felt a chill as he remembered what had happened

to her and her family last spring. Some crazy woman had pretended to be a long-lost cousin, and having designs on Hud, had tried to kill Dana, her children and her best friend, Hilde. Fortunately Deputy Colt Dawson had found out the woman's true identity and arrived in time to save them all.

Tag couldn't imagine something so horrifying, but if anything, his cousin Dana was resilient and Camilla Northland was in prison, where hopefully she would remain the rest of her life.

The new snow higher up the mountain was as light as down feathers and floated around him as he climbed. He had to stop a couple of times to catch his breath because of the altitude. "You're not in Texas anymore," he said, laughing.

The land flattened out some once he was near the top, and he knew he'd hit the old logging road. As he started down it, he kept looking for the perfect tree. Dana's husband, Marshal Hud Savage, had warned him not to let Dana come back with one of her "orphan" trees. Hud hadn't been able to come along with them. He was working on a burglary case involving a condo break-in and a possible missing person.

"She'll find a tree that she knows no one will ever cut because it's so pitiful and she'll want to give it a Christmas," Hud warned him. "Don't let her. You should see some of the trees that woman has brought home."

Tag told himself he would be happy with whatever tree they found as long as it was evergreen. But he knew he was looking for something special. He hadn't had a real Christmas tree in years. Along with getting one for Dana's living room, he planned to pick up a small one for his father's cabin. He knew Harlan probably didn't decorate for Christmas, but he'd have to put up with it this year since his son was determined to spend Christmas with him.

Dana had said she would lend them some ornaments and the kids would make some, as well. Tag couldn't wait, he thought, as he looked around for a large pretty tree for Dana and a smaller version for him and his father.

He hadn't gone far down the logging road when he picked up a snowmobile track coming in from what appeared to be another old logging road. Dana had told him that they often had trouble in the winter with snowmobilers on the property because of the catacomb of logging roads that ran for miles.

He remembered hearing one late last night, now that he thought about it. A lot of people got around that way in the wintertime. For all he knew, his father had been out and about after the bar closed. To visit his girl-friend? The thought made him smile.

"I found a tree!" Dana called from somewhere below him on the mountain. He couldn't see her through the thick, snow-filled pines.

"An orphan tree?" he called back, and heard her laugh. "Hud will have my head," he mumbled to himself as he started to drop off the side of the mountain, heading in the direction he'd heard Dana laugh.

He'd only taken a couple of steps when the sun caught on an object off to his right. Tag saw what looked like a branch sticking up out of the snow. Only there was something very odd about the branch. It was blue.

As he stepped closer, his heart leapt to his throat. It wasn't a branch.

A hand, frosty in the morning sun, stuck up out of the deep snow.

MARSHAL HUD SAVAGE arrived by snowmobile thirty minutes after he'd gotten the call from his wife. He found Dana and Tag standing half a dozen yards away from the body. It was the second time in the past six years that remains had been found on the ranch. Hud could see that Dana was upset and worried.

"It's going to be all right," he told her. "Go on down to the house and wait for the coroner. He'll need directions up here."

As soon as she left, he stooped down and brushed the snow off the victim's face. Behind him, Tag let out a startled sound, making him turn.

"You know her?" he asked.

Tag nodded, but he seemed to need a minute to find his voice. "She works at the Canyon," he said finally. "I think her name is Mia. I ran into her at the bar last night. Or more correctly, she ran into me. Was she… *murdered?*"

"Looks like she was strangled with the scarf around her neck," Hud said. He could see where the scarf had cut into her throat. "But we'll know more once the coroner and the lab does the autopsy."

"I thought it might have been an accident," Tag said.

Hud studied him. He seemed awfully shaken for a man who'd only just run into the woman the night before. "So, what exactly happened last night at the bar?"

He listened while Tag recounted the woman stumbling into him, apparently quite drunk, and how he'd gone out the back door after her to make sure she was all right. "I saw her getting into a pickup with a man."

"And you think her name was Mia?" Hud asked. Could this be the missing Mia Duncan? He had a bad feeling it was.

Tag told him that all he knew was what another

server at the Canyon had told him. "She had apparently left in the middle of her shift."

"Do you know the name of the other server you talked to?"

"Lily. At least that's what the bartender called her."

Hud nodded. "Tell me about the man the victim left with behind the bar."

"Cowboy hat, pickup. It was snowing so hard I can't even swear what color the truck was. Dark blue or brown, maybe even black. That's about it. I only got a glimpse of the man through the snow," Tag said.

"But he got a good look at you?"

He saw that the question took Tag by surprise. "Yeah, I guess he did."

"I might need a statement from you later," Hud said. "If you think of anything else…"

"I'll let you know," Tag said as the coroner and another deputy arrived by snowmobile. The coroner's had a sled behind his snowmobile.

"Dana will have a pot of coffee on when you reach the house," Hud told him. He'd seen Tag's rented SUV parked in front of the ranch house.

Tag nodded and turned to leave.

Hud watched him go, worrying. Dana had just been disappointed by one "cousin." He didn't want her disappointed again if he could help it. But he couldn't shake the feeling that Tanner "Tag" Cardwell knew a lot more about the victim than he'd admitted.

He reminded himself that his instincts were off. He was probably just looking for guilt where there wasn't any.

TAG WAS GLAD he didn't have to talk to anyone on the walk down the mountain. His head was spinning.

He'd been shocked when he'd recognized the dead woman—even more shocked when he'd seen what she was wearing. A leather jacket like the one he'd seen lying over the arm of his father's couch just yesterday.

Since discovering the body, he'd kept telling himself it couldn't be the same woman. Just as his father couldn't be involved in this.

That was why he hadn't mentioned the jacket to the marshal, he told himself. He couldn't be sure it was the same one. But both his father and the woman had been at the bar last night. Tag knew how some women were about cowboy guitar players—even old ones.

A chill had settled in his bones by the time he reached the ranch house. He liked the idea of a hot cup of coffee, but he didn't want to talk to anyone—especially his cousin—about what he'd seen on the mountain.

As he climbed into his rented SUV, he told himself that the woman's death had nothing to do with his father. And yet Tag couldn't wait to reach the cabin. Harlan Cardwell had some explaining to do.

LILY TRIED NOT to roll her eyes at her brother. *"Ace."*

"Don't 'Ace' me. Lily, it's time you got back on the horse. So to speak."

She really didn't want to talk about this and now regretted stopping by her brother's tiny apartment over the bar this early in the morning. She'd come to talk about Mia Duncan—not her ex-fiancé, Gerald Humphrey.

"What chaps my behind is that Gerald was the wrong man for you in the first place," Ace said as he refilled her coffee cup. "That man would have bored you to death in no time."

She thought about how much she and Gerald had

in common. Of course Ace thought him boring. Ace had never understood what she and Gerald had shared.

"But to pull what he did," Ace continued. "If he hadn't skipped the country when he did, I would have tracked him down and—"

"I really don't want to have this discussion," she said, picking up her mug and moving over to the window. The world was covered in cold white drifts this morning. The sun had come out, turning the fresh snow to a blinding carpet of diamonds.

"Sis, I love you and I hate to see you like this."

Lily spun back around, almost spilling her coffee. She couldn't help being annoyed with the older brother she'd idolized all her life. But this was a subject they had never agreed on.

"You hate to see me like *this?*" she demanded. "Ace, I'm *happy.* I have a great life, a rewarding career. I'm… content."

He mugged a face. "Sis, you live like a nun except for the few times a year that I drag you out to help me with the bar."

"We really should not have this conversation," she warned him, wondering now if he had actually needed her help at the bar or if his asking her to work the holidays with him was part of some scheme to find her a man. If it was the latter… She said as much. "Ace, so help me—"

He held up his hands in surrender. "You know how much I need your help. And I didn't mean to set you off this morning."

But he had. "You should be more concerned about your *other* employees. If you had seen Mia's condo…"

"I *am* concerned. I put in a call to the marshal's office first thing this morning, but no one has called me back yet. I called the condo number Mia gave me, but not surprisingly, there was no answer there. I figure once she discovered the break-in, she probably stayed with a friend last night."

Lily wasn't so sure about that since she didn't think Mia had made any friends in the weeks she'd been working at the Canyon. The only person Mia had spoken to at the bar was Teresa. Which had seemed odd because of the age difference.

Mia was in her late thirties, while Teresa was barely twenty-one. Neither was outgoing, so that could be why they'd become somewhat friends, at least from Lily's observation.

So this morning, she'd placed a call to Teresa's cell, only to reach her boyfriend, Ethan. "Mia isn't the only one who's missing this morning," she told her brother. "That's why I came by so early. Teresa didn't come home last night."

Ace seemed only a little surprised, but then he'd been running a bar longer than Lily had been helping out. "Maybe Mia and Teresa are together. I'm sure they'll turn up. Teresa and Ethan probably had a fight. I noticed she was acting oddly last night." He frowned. "But then again, so was Mia, now that I think about it. I saw her get into it with one of the customers. Teresa came to her rescue, but Mia handled it fine."

"Why didn't you tell me about that last night?" Lily demanded.

"Because it blew over quickly. You and Reggie didn't even notice."

"Who was the customer?"

Ace shrugged. "Some guy. I didn't recognize him. Lily, people act up in bars. It happens. A good server knows how to handle it. Mia was great. I'm telling you,

I wouldn't be surprised if they both show up for work tonight."

Lily hoped he was right. "Did you ask Mia why she left early night before last?"

"She apologized, said she'd suddenly gotten a migraine and hadn't been able to get my attention, but since it hadn't been that busy…"

Lily nodded. Had Mia been drinking the night before last as well as last night? If so, Lily really hadn't seen that coming.

But what did she really know about the woman? Other servers she'd worked with often talked about their lives—in detail—while they were setting up before opening and cleaning up after closing. She'd learned more than she'd ever wanted to know about them.

Mia, though, was another story. She seldom offered anything about herself other than where she was from— Billings, Montana, the largest city in the state and a good three hours away. It wasn't unusual for people from Billings to have condos at Big Sky. Mia's parents owned a condo in one of the pricier developments, which made Lily suspect that the woman didn't really need this job.

"What do you know about Mia?" Lily asked her brother now.

He shrugged. "Not much. She never had much to say, especially about herself. I could check her application, but you know there isn't a lot on them."

"But there would be a number to call in case of emergency, right?"

"I think that is more than a little premature," her brother said. "Anyway, if the marshal thought that was necessary, he would have contacted me for the number, right?"

"Maybe. Unless they have some rule about not looking for a missing adult for twenty-four hours. Still, I'd like to see her job application."

Ace got to his feet. "I've got to open the bar soon anyway. Come on."

In the Canyon office, her brother pulled out Mia Duncan's application from the file cabinet and handed it to her.

He was right. There was little on the form other than name, address, social security number, local phone number and an emergency contact number. Most of his employees were temporary hires, usually college students attending Montana State University forty miles down the highway to the north, and only stayed a few weeks at most. Big Sky had a fairly transient population that came and went by the season.

So Lily wasn't surprised that the number Mia had put down on her application was a local number, probably her parents' condo here at Big Sky.

"No cell phone number," she said. "That's odd since I've seen Mia using a cell phone on at least one of her breaks behind the bar."

Lily didn't recognize the prefix on the emergency number Mia had put down. She picked up the phone and dialed it, ignoring her brother shaking his head in disapproval. The number rang three times before a voice came on the line to say the phone had been disconnected.

"What?" Ace asked as she hung up.

"The number's been disconnected. I'll call the condo association." A few moments later she hung up, now more upset and worried than before. "That condo doesn't belong to her parents. It belongs to a retired FBI agent who recently died. The condo association didn't even know Mia was staying there."

At a loud knock at the bar's front door, they both started. Lily glanced out the office window and felt her heart drop at the sight of the marshal's pickup.

Chapter Four

As Tag pulled up in front of his father's cabin, he saw that Harlan's SUV was gone. He hadn't seen much of his father since he'd arrived and wasn't all that surprised to find the cabin empty. Harlan had been in bed this morning when Tag had left to go Christmas tree hunting. He had the feeling that his father didn't spend much time here.

Tag felt too antsy to sit around and wait. He needed Harlan to put his mind at ease. That leather jacket the dead woman was wearing was a dead ringer for the one he'd seen on the arm of Harlan's couch.

Fortunately, he had a pretty good idea where to find his father. If Harlan Cardwell was anything, he was predictable. At least Tag had always thought that was true. Now, thinking about the murdered woman, he wasn't so sure.

Just as he'd suspected, though, he found his father at the Corral Bar down the canyon. Harlan was sitting on a bar stool next to his brother, Angus. A song about men, their dogs and their women was playing on the jukebox.

The sight of the two Cardwell men sitting there brought back memories of when Tag was a boy. Some men felt more at home in a bar than in their own house.

Harlan Cardwell was one of them. His brother, Angus, was another.

Tag studied the two of them for a moment. It hit him that he didn't know his father and might never get to know him. Harlan definitely hadn't made an attempt over the years. Tag couldn't see that changing on this visit—even if his father had nothing to do with the dead woman.

"Hey, Tag," Uncle Angus said, spotting him just inside the doorway. He slid off his bar stool to shake Tag's hand. "You sure grew up."

Tag had to laugh, since he'd been twelve when he'd left the canyon, the eldest of his brothers. Now he stood six-two, broad across the shoulders and slim at the hips—much as his father had been in his early thirties.

After his mother had packed up her five boys and said goodbye to their father and the canyon for good, they'd seen Harlan occasionally for very short visits when their mother had insisted he fly down to Texas for one event in his boys' lives or another.

"I hope you stopped by to have a drink with us," Tag's uncle said.

Tag glanced at the clock behind the bar, shocked it was almost noon. The two older men looked pretty chipper considering they'd closed down the Canyon Bar last night. They'd both been too handsome in their youths for their own good. Since then they'd aged surprisingly well. He could see where a younger woman might be attracted to his father.

Harlan had never remarried. Nor had his brother. Tag had thought that neither of them probably even dated. He'd always believed that both men were happiest either on a stage with guitars in their hands or on a bar stool side by side in some canyon bar.

But he could be wrong about that. He could be wrong about a lot of things.

"I'm not sure Tag drinks," his father said to Angus, and glanced toward the front door as if expecting someone.

Angus laughed. "He's a Cardwell. He *has* to drink," he said, and motioned to the bartender.

"I'll have a beer," Tag said, standing next to his uncle. "Whatever is on tap will be fine."

Angus slapped him on the back and laughed. "This is my nephew," he told the bartender. "Set him up."

Several patrons down the bar were talking about the declining elk herds and blaming the reintroduction of wolves. Tag half expected the talk at the bar would be about the young cocktail waitress's death, but apparently Hud had been able to keep a lid on it for the time being.

Tag realized he couldn't put this off any longer. "Could we step outside?" he asked his father. "I need to talk to you in private for a moment."

"It's cold outside," Harlan said, frowning as he glanced toward the front door of the bar again. Snow had been plowed into a wall of white at the edge of the parking area. Ice crystals floated in the cold late-morning air. "If this can't wait, we could step into the back room, I guess."

"Fine." Tag could tell his father was reluctant to leave the bar. He seemed to be watching the front door. Who was he expecting? The woman who'd been in his cabin yesterday?

"So, what's up?" his father asked the moment Tag closed the door behind them.

"I need to ask you something. Who was at your cabin yesterday when I showed up unexpectedly?" Tag asked.

"I told you there wasn't—"

"I saw her leather jacket on the couch."

Harlan met his gaze. "My personal life isn't—"

"A woman wearing a jacket exactly like that one was just found murdered on the Cardwell Ranch."

Shock registered in his father's face—but only for an instant.

That instant was long enough, though, that Tag's stomach had time to fall. "I know you couldn't have had anything to do with her murder—"

"Of course not," Harlan snapped. "I don't even know the woman."

Tag stared at his father. "How could you know that, since I haven't told you her name?"

"Because the woman who owns the leather jacket you saw at my cabin came by right after you left this morning. She is alive and well."

Tag let out a relieved sigh. "Good. I just had to check before I said anything to the marshal."

"Well, I'm glad of that."

"I had to ask because this woman is the same one who stumbled into me last night at the Canyon—the same bar where you and Uncle Angus were playing. After seeing that leather jacket at your cabin…well, you can see why I jumped to conclusions."

"I suppose so," his father said, frowning. "Let's have that beer now. We'll be lucky if your uncle hasn't drank them."

"The woman worked at the Canyon Bar," Tag said, wondering why his father hadn't asked. Big Sky was a small community—at least off-season. Wouldn't he have been curious as to who'd been murdered? "She was working last night while you were playing in the band.

A tall blonde woman? I'm sure you must have noticed her. Her name was Mia."

Harlan looked irritated. "I told you—"

"Right. You don't know her." He opened the door and followed his father back to the bar. Angus was talking to the bartender. Their beers hadn't been touched.

The last thing Tag wanted right now was alcohol. His stomach felt queasy, but he knew he couldn't leave without drinking at least some of it. He didn't look at his father as he took a gulp of his beer. He couldn't look at him. His father's reaction had rocked him to his core. A young woman was murdered last night, her body dumped from a snowmobile on an old logging road on the Cardwell Ranch. He kept seeing his father's first reaction—that instant when he couldn't hide his shock and pretend disinterest.

"You two doing all right?" Angus asked, glancing first at Tag, then at Harlan. Neither of them had spoken since they'd returned to the bar. Tag saw a look pass between the brothers. Angus reached for his beer and took a long drink.

Tag picked up his, taking a couple more gulps as he watched his father and uncle out of the corner of his eye. Some kind of message had passed between them. Neither looked happy.

"I'm sorry but I need to get going," he said, checking his watch. "I'm meeting someone." He'd never been good at lying, but when he looked up he saw that neither his father nor his uncle was paying any attention. Nor did they try to detain him. If anything, they seemed relieved that he was leaving.

Biting down on his fear that his father had just lied to him, he reached for his wallet.

"Put that away," his uncle said. "Your money is no good here."

"Thanks." He looked past Angus at his father. "I guess I'll see you later?"

"I'm sure you will," Harlan said.

"Dana's having us all out Christmas Eve," Tag said. "You're planning to be there, aren't you?"

"I wouldn't miss it for anything," his father said. He hadn't looked toward the door even once since they'd returned from the back room.

Tag felt his chest tighten as he left the bar. Once out in his rented SUV, he debated what to do. All his instincts told him to go to the marshal. But what if he was wrong? What if his father was telling the truth? He couldn't chance alienating his father further if he was wrong.

On a hunch, he pulled around the building out of sight and waited. Just as he suspected, his father and uncle came out of the bar not five minutes later. They said something to each other as they parted, both looking unhappy, then headed for their respective rigs before heading down the canyon toward Big Sky.

Tag let them both get ahead of him before he pulled out and followed. He doubted his father would recognize the rented SUV he was driving. It looked like a lot of other SUVs, so nondescript it didn't stand out in the least. He stayed back anyway, just far enough he could keep them in sight.

His uncle turned off on the road to his cabin on the river, but Harlan kept going. Tag planned to follow his father all the way to Big Sky but was surprised when Harlan turned into the Cardwell Ranch instead. Tag hung back until his father's SUV dropped over a rise; then he, too, turned into the ranch. Within sight of the old two-story farmhouse, Tag pulled over in a stand of pines.

Through the snow-laden pine boughs, he could see his father and the marshal standing outside by Hud's patrol car. They appeared to be arguing. At one point, he saw Hud point back up into the mountains—in the direction where Tag had found the dead woman's body. Then he saw his father pull out an envelope and hand it to the marshal. Hud looked angry and resisted taking it for a moment, but then quickly stuffed it under his jacket, looking around as if worried they had been seen.

Tag couldn't breathe. He told himself he couldn't have seen what he thought he had. His imagination was running wild. Had that been some kind of payoff?

A few minutes later, his father climbed back into his SUV and headed out of the ranch.

Tag hurriedly turned around and left, his mind racing. What had that been about? There was no doubt in his mind it had something to do with the dead woman his father had denied knowing.

DANA STARED AT the Christmas tree, fighting tears.

"It's not *that* ugly," her sister, Stacy, said from the couch.

Last night, Dana, her husband and her two oldest children had decorated it. It hadn't taken long, since the poor tree had very few limbs. Hud had just stared at it and sighed. Mary, five, and Hank, six, had declared it beautiful.

Never a crier except when she was pregnant and her hormones were raging, Dana burst into tears. Her sister got up, put an arm around her and walked her over to the couch to sit down next to her.

"Is it postpartum depression?" Stacy asked.

She shook her head. "It's Hud. I'm afraid for him."

"You knew he was a marshal when you married him," her sister pointed out, looking confused.

"He's talking about quitting."

Stacy blinked in surprise. "He loves being a marshal."

"*Loved.* After what happened here on the ranch last spring, he doesn't think he has what it takes anymore."

"That's ridiculous." A woman pretending to be their cousin had turned out to be a psychopathic con artist. "Camilla fooled us all."

Dana sniffed. "Not Hilde." Her sister handed her a tissue. Hilde had tried to warn her, but she'd thought her best friend was just being jealous and hadn't taken her worries seriously. Not taking Hilde's warnings seriously had almost gotten them killed.

"Hilde's forgiven you, right?" Stacy asked as Dana wiped her eyes and blew her nose.

"Kind of. I mean, she says she has. But, Stacy, I took some stranger's word over my best friend's, who is also my business partner and godmother to one of my children!"

"You and Hud both need to let this go. Camilla is locked up in the women's state prison in Billings, right? With six counts of attempted murder, she won't get out until she's ninety."

"What if she pretends to be reformed and gets out on good behavior? Or worse, escapes? We're only a few hours away."

"You can't really think she's going to escape."

"If anyone can, it's her. Within a week, I'll bet she was eating her meals with the warden. You know how she is."

"Dana, you're making her into the bogeyman. She's just a sick woman with a lot of scars."

Dana looked at Stacy. Her older sister had her own scars from bad marriages, worse relationships and some really horrible choices she'd made. But since she'd had her daughter, Ella, Stacy had truly changed.

"I'm so glad you're in my life again," Dana said to her sister, and hugged Stacy hard.

"Me, too." Stacy frowned. "You have to let what happened go."

Dana nodded, but she knew that was easier said than done. "I have nightmares about her. I think Hud does, too. I can't shake the feeling that Camilla isn't out of our lives."

CAMILLA NORTHLAND WAS surprised how easy it was for her to adapt to prison. She spent her days working out in the prison weight room, and after a month of hitting it hard, figured she was in the best shape of her life.

She'd tuned in to how things went in prison right away. It reminded her of high school. That was why she picked the biggest, meanest woman she could find, went up to her and punched her in the face. She'd lost the fight since the woman was too big and strong for her.

But ultimately she'd won the war. Other prisoners gave her a wide berth. Stories began to circulate about her, some of them actually true. She'd heard whispers that everyone thought she was half-crazy.

Only half?

Like the other inmates, she already had a nickname, Spark. Camilla could only assume it was because of the arson conviction that had been tacked on to her attempted murder convictions.

She'd skipped a long trial, confessed and pleaded

guilty, speeding up the process that would ultimately land her in prison anyway. It wasn't as though any judge in his right mind was going to allow her bail. Nor did she want the publicity of a trial that she feared, once it went nationwide, would bring her other misdeeds to light.

The local papers had run stories about the fire and Dana and her babies and best friend barely escaping. Dana and Hilde had become heroes.

It was enough to make Camilla puke.

So now she was Spark. Over the years she'd gone by so many different names that she was fine with Spark. She liked to think that whoever had given her the new moniker had realized she was always just a spark away from blowing sky-high.

She knew that if she was going to survive, let alone thrive here, she had to be in the right group. That, too, was so much like high school, it made her laugh.

The group she wanted to run with had to be not just the most fearsome but also the ones who ran this prison. She might be locked up, but she wasn't done with Hud Savage and his precious family. Not by a long shot.

Being behind bars would make it harder, though, she had to admit. But she knew there were ways to get what she wanted. What she wanted was vengeance.

So the moment she heard about fellow prisoner Edna Mable Jones, or Grams as she was fondly called, Camilla knew she would have it.

TAG HADN'T REALIZED where he was going until he saw the sign over the front door. The Canyon. As he pulled up in front of the bar, the door swung open and the barmaid he'd met the night before stepped out and headed for an SUV parked nearby. He figured that by now Hud would have talked to her and anyone else at the bar who'd known the victim.

Earlier, he'd told himself there was nothing he could do but wait for the marshal to catch the killer. That was before he'd talked to his father—and witnessed the meeting between Hud and Harlan at Cardwell Ranch. As much as he didn't want to believe his father was involved, he knew in his heart that Harlan was up to his neck in this. He was more shocked that it appeared the marshal was involved, as well.

As he watched the brunette head for her SUV, he realized he'd come here because he'd hoped Lily would be able to help him. She had worked with the dead woman. She also might know something about Harlan since apparently the Canyon Cowboys had played at the bar on more than one occasion.

She had started to climb into her vehicle, but when she saw him, she stopped. Frowning, she slammed the door and marched over to Tag's rental SUV.

"You," she said as he put down his side window. "I just told the marshal about you and how you were the last one to see Mia."

He laughed, clearly surprising her. "Other than the killer. Also, the marshal already knows about me. Hud Savage is my cousin-in-law. I'm the one who found her body."

Lily pulled back, startled. *"You?"*

Tag hadn't heard the bartender from last night come out of the bar until he spoke. "Lily, you're starting to sound like an owl," he said as he joined them.

"This is the man I told you about," she said to the bartender. "The one who said Mia was drunk." She narrowed her eyes when she looked at Tag again, accusation in her tone and every muscle of her nicely rounded body. "He *claims* he's related to the marshal."

The bartender shook his head at Lily and reached past her to extend his hand. "James McCabe, but everyone around here knows me as Ace. You must be one of Harlan's sons, right?"

"Tag Cardwell."

"Cardwell?" Lily said in surprise.

"This is my sister, Lily, but I guess you two have met." Ace seemed amused.

Then his sister said, "He found Mia."

Ace nodded somberly. "We're in shock. In fact, I just put a note on the door that we're going to be closed tonight. We didn't know Mia that well, but the least we can do is close for the night in her memory." He glanced at his watch. "I told the marshal I would stop by his office. I better get going." He squeezed his sister's shoulder and said, "Nice to meet you," to Tag before he walked over to an old Jeep and climbed in.

Neither Tag nor Lily spoke until her brother had driven away.

"Sorry about—"

Tag waved her apology away. "You don't know me from Adam. I would have been disappointed if you hadn't suspected me."

She narrowed her eyes at him again as she realized he was flirting with her. "Have you remembered any more about the man Mia left with last night?" she asked, all business.

He shook his head. "I wish I'd gotten a better look at him or paid more attention to the truck he was driving." But it had been snowing hard and he'd had no reason to pay that much attention.

"I can't believe anyone would murder her."

He nodded, thinking what a shock murder was in a place like Big Sky. Crime was so low people felt safe here. When he was young, he and his brothers were allowed to wander all over this country. Looking back, he knew there'd been a fair share of close calls while climbing rocks, swimming in the river, skiing and sledding off the side of mountains. But they'd never known the kind of danger the dead woman had run across.

"You said you didn't think she had a boyfriend, right? Did you ever see her talking with someone in the bar she might have had an interest in?" *Like a member of the band,* but he didn't say that.

"No one she seemed interested in. She just did her job. I never even saw her flirting with anyone. So maybe she did have a boyfriend. She didn't talk about her personal life." Lily sighed and started to walk to her vehicle again.

"Lily?" He liked the name and it seemed to fit her.

She turned to look at him over her shoulder, leery again.

"If you ever want to talk, or maybe…" He dug in his coat pocket, thinking he might have one of his business cards. When he felt something odd shaped, cold and hard, he frowned and drew it out. "What the…?"

Lily stepped back to his open window. "What's wrong?"

"This," he said, holding up the object he'd found. "I don't know what it is."

"It's a computer thumb drive," she said, then eyed him as if she thought he was messing with her.

"I know that," he said. "The question is, what is it doing in my coat pocket? I have no idea how it got there."

"When was the last time you checked your pockets?" she asked.

He shrugged. "I bought this ski jacket before I flew out here. Yesterday was the first time I've worn it."

She frowned. "Are you saying it wasn't in your pocket when you left Texas?"

"I don't know. I don't think so. All I can tell you is that it isn't mine." He tried to remember where his ski jacket had been. Last night at the cabin, his father had taken his coat and hung it up. Was it possible he'd put the thumb drive in the pocket? Why would he do that?

With a start, Tag remembered the dead cocktail waitress stumbling into him, grabbing his coat and holding on to him as he tried to help her get her feet under her. A chill ran the length of his spine as he remembered her words.

"You look like him."

Was it possible she meant Harlan?

Before he could shove the thought away, Lily said, "Is there any chance Mia put it in your pocket last night?"

Chapter Five

"I think we'd better see what's on that thumb drive," Lily said. "There's a computer in the bar office." With that she turned and headed for the front door. She heard Tag Cardwell come up behind her as she inserted her key into the lock.

"Why would she put this in my pocket?"

Lily shook her head. She had no idea. Just as she had no idea why Mia had left early two nights in a row or why Tag had thought Mia was falling-down drunk. She said as much as she opened the door to the bar, locking it behind them, before leading him to the office.

"Isn't it possible she was pretending to be drunk?" Lily asked, although that seemed even more far-fetched.

"She wasn't pretending," Tag said.

"Then she got drunk awfully fast after I talked to her." Stepping behind the desk, she held out her hand for the thumb drive.

"She smelled boozy, but it could have been drugs."

Lily shook her head. "Not Mia." But even as she said it, she realized again how little she really knew about the woman.

"You know, I was just thinking," he said as he handed over the thumb drive with obvious reluctance. "It's possible one of my brothers put it in my pocket at the airport as I was leaving. We're in business together, so it could be tax information they wanted me to look at. My brother and my nephew saw me off at the airport. In fact, my brother held my coat while I was looking for my ticket."

She could tell he wanted the thumb drive to turn out to be something simple and innocent. No one wanted to think they had any kind of connection to a young woman's murder. She figured he was probably right. The other was too much like a spy movie.

As she considered Tag, she had to admit he would make a great spy. He looked like the kind of man who could save the damsel in distress. He definitely was sure of himself. But a spy with a Stetson and a Texas accent? It had more appeal than she wanted to admit, and she quickly shook the image off.

Lately her mind had been wandering into the strangest places. She knew what her brother would have to say about it. He was determined she find another man after what she liked to think of as "the Gerald Era" with its straight-out-of-a-country-and-western-song bad ending.

She pushed in the thumb drive, and Tag came around the end of the desk to stand next to her. He smelled like winter, a blend of cold and pine. She ignored the masculine scent just below the surface as she ignored the way her nerve endings jumped with him standing so close. Maybe her brother was right and it was time to get back on that horse that had thrown her.

It was definitely time to quit the cowboy clichés.

The icon came up on the page. She hesitated only a moment before she clicked on it. A series of random letters appeared.

GUHA BKOPAR
CAKNCA IKKNA

BNWJG IKKJAU
HSQ SWUJA
YHAPA NWJZ
NWU AIANU

LWQH XNKSJ
IEW ZQJYWJ
YWH BNWJGHEJ
HWNO HWJZANO
DWNHWJ YWNZSAHH
DQZ OWRWCA

"It's just gibberish," Tag said with a relieved laugh. "It looks like some kid was playing on a computer."

Lily nodded, feeling disappointed. "It does look that way," she agreed. She checked, but this page was the only thing on the thumb drive.

She'd wanted answers so desperately about Mia that she'd latched on to the thumb drive, determined she could solve the mystery. It was the way she approached life, her brother would have told her. Full steam ahead— as long as it was logical. The thumb drive hadn't been the answer, nor had she jumped to the logical conclusion. It wasn't like her.

Tag stepped away, shaking his head. "Maybe it was something my nephew put in my pocket. Ford's five and is always playing on the computer. He was at the airport with his dad the day I flew out."

"You're suggesting your five-year-old nephew put this on a thumb drive for you?" she asked skeptically.

"It's probably his idea of a goodbye letter. My brother would have put it on the thumb drive for him. Jackson is a single parent," he said as if that explained it enough for him.

Lily wasn't as convinced. Admittedly, she'd been so sure Mia had put it in his coat pocket last night that she hated to give up the possibility. How nice it would have been if whatever was on the thumb drive would provide a clue to the woman's murder. Unfortunately the world seldom worked the way she thought it should.

"I was wondering," Tag said. "Since the bar won't be open tonight..."

His words didn't register until much later. Lily was busy staring at the letters on the screen trying to make them into more than they no doubt were.

The fact that the letters were all capitalized substantiated Tag's theory that they were probably done by a child who had just happened to hit Caps Lock before he started typing.

What interested her was that the lines were so short—none more than fourteen letters. The columns were also short, one on top of the other, broken halfway down by an empty line, then an equal number of lines below that. Six each. Awfully neat for a child, she thought, but then it could have been random—just like the letters.

She mentioned this to Tag without looking away from the screen.

"You *counted* them?" He laughed, then sobered when she sent him a withering look. "Sorry, it just seems odd to me that you'd count them."

Lily tried not to let his comment annoy her. "I'm a mathematician. I tend to count things."

His dark eyes widened. "A *mathematician?*"

She could tell he was fighting a grin, hoping she was joking. "I teach math at Montana State University," she said simply. Lily had seen too many men's eyes glaze over when she'd tried to explain her love of mathematics or how important it was for solving economic, scientific, engineering and business problems. Few people realized they used math in so many ways in their daily lives. Nor did they care, for that matter.

"Oh," was all he said. Much better than the men who said, "So you're smart." After that, they quit calling.

"Would you mind if I kept this for now?" she asked, pointing at the thumb drive.

Tag shrugged. "It's all yours. I'll check with my brother, but I'm betting my nephew Ford is behind this." Clearly, he was no longer worried about it. "I could call you later and let you know."

Lily realized that earlier he'd been about to ask her something about tonight. Had he been about to ask her on a date? She hadn't dated since Gerald. The thought of going out with this cowboy—

"I'll need your number," he said.

"So you can let me know what your brother says about the thumb drive. Right."

"Right," he said, looking amused at how flustered she had become.

She scribbled her number on one of the Canyon Bar business cards and handed it to him. Then she saved the page to the computer, emailed herself a copy, ejected the thumb drive and stood holding it.

"You sure you don't mind me keeping this for now?"

He grinned. "No problem. If it is a letter from my nephew, well, I think I got the gist of it," he said with a laugh.

And if it wasn't? She pocketed the thumb drive before walking him to the door. Ace had made a sign he'd posted, saying because of a death, the bar would be closed for the day. It was taped to the door as she let Tag out.

He seemed to hesitate before heading to his SUV. "I'm sorry about Mia."

"Thank you. Let me know what your brother says about the thumb drive."

Tag nodded and looked as if he had more he wanted to say, but after a moment, he touched his cowboy hat and left.

TAG HAD ALMOST asked Lily McCabe out. Mentally he kicked himself as he climbed behind the wheel of the SUV. Lily had lost a woman she'd worked with. She probably wasn't interested in going out with the man who'd found the victim's body. Not tonight anyway.

There'd be another chance before he left, he mused. He just hoped she didn't think the reason he hadn't pursued it was that she taught math. Wouldn't she have to have a PhD to teach math at a university? He let out a low whistle that came out frosty white in the winter air. Beautiful *and* smart. Everything about Lily McCabe intrigued him.

The temperature was dropping fast, but he hadn't noticed until he sat down on the pickup seat. It was as cold as a block of ice, hard as one, too.

He got the engine going. The heater was blowing freezing-cold air. He turned it off until the engine warmed up, rubbing his hands together. Even with gloves on, his fingers ached. He really should have gone with the more expensive rental—the one with the heated seats. But he was a Texas boy who'd forgotten how cold it got up here in Montana.

When he reached his father's cabin, he saw that Harlan hadn't returned. He couldn't imagine where he might have gone, so he went inside to wait. Lily Mc-Cabe had taken his thoughts off his father and his growing suspicions. But now, standing in his father's empty cabin, they were back with a vengeance.

He desperately wanted to believe that Hud would find the killer and clear all this up. Unfortunately, he kept picturing his father handing the marshal the thick envelope. What the hell was going on?

At the window, he caught a glimpse of Lone Mountain looming against the cold blue sky and thought about going skiing. But he felt too antsy. Maybe his father had gone over to Uncle Angus's.

As he started to leave the cabin, he remembered his promise to call his brother. He dialed Jackson's number and was relieved when he answered on the third ring.

"How's Montana?" his brother asked.

Tag thought it telling that Jackson hadn't asked how their father was first. "It's beautiful. Cold and snowy. I'm thinking about heading up to the ski hill." Not quite true, but it sounded good.

Jackson laughed. "Glad I'm in sunny, warm Texas, then."

"As the youngest, you probably don't have the great memories I do of the canyon. But this place grows on you. Summers here are better than any place on earth."

"How's Harlan?" Jackson and their brothers had quit calling him Dad a long time ago.

Tag wasn't sure how to answer that. "I went down to this local bar last night and listened to him and Uncle Angus play in their band. He really is a damned good guitar player. Mom might have been right about him having a chance at the big time."

"Yeah, right," Jackson said, clearly losing interest in this part of the conversation. His brother had thought he was a fool to want to spend Christmas with their father—let alone surprise him.

"You know how he is," Jackson had said. "I just hate to see you get hurt."

"I'm not expecting anything," Tag had said, but he could tell his brother didn't believe him. As the eldest, he had the most memories. He'd missed his father.

He realized that he'd had more expectations than he had wanted to admit. He'd wanted Harlan to be glad to see him. He'd also wanted Harlan to act like a caring father. So far he was batting zero.

"I need to ask you a question," Tag said. "When you and Ford saw me off at the airport, did Ford put a thumb drive in my pocket?"

"You mean one of those computer flash drives?"

Tag felt his heart drop. "I thought maybe he'd written me a goodbye letter on the computer and you saved it to one since I found one in my pocket."

"You do know that Ford is five and doesn't know how to write goodbye letters, right?"

"Yeah, but what's on the thumb drive looks like a kid typed it, pretending he was writing a goodbye letter."

"Sorry, I had nothing to do with it, but I'll ask Ford if he knows anything about it." He left the phone, returning a few moments later. "Nope. Ford's innocent. At least this time," he added with a laugh. "So, when are you coming back?"

"I'm not sure." Earlier he'd told his uncle he was leaving right after Christmas. That was before he'd officially met Lily McCabe. "Probably after New Year's."

"Hope you solve the mystery of the thumb drive," Jackson said with a laugh.

"I'm sure it's nothing." He thought of Mia and his father. He hoped to hell it was nothing.

LILY PUT THE thumb drive into her laptop the moment she got to her house. The house was small by Big Sky standards—only three bedrooms, three baths, a restaurant-quality kitchen, a large formal dining room and an open living room with a high-beamed ceiling.

The structure sat back into the trees against the mountainside and had a large deck at the front with a nice porch area next to the driveway and garage. She'd chosen simple furnishings, a leather couch in butter-scotch, her mother's old wooden rocker, a couple of club chairs with antique quilts thrown over them.

The dining room table was large, the chairs comfortable. It was right off the kitchen and living room. That was where she kept her computer because she liked the view. She was high enough on the mountain that she could look out through the large windows at the front of the house and see one of the many ski hills and the mountains beyond. It felt as if she could see forever.

The moment she inserted the flash drive, the letters came up again on the screen. It looked like a foreign language, one with a lot of hard vowels.

She knew she didn't want the letters to be random and that she was going to be disappointed if Tag was right and they were just gibberish typed in by a child.

But as she pulled up a chair, she thought about Mia. What if she was the one who'd put this thumb drive in Tag's jacket pocket—just as her imaginative mind had suggested? He'd said that Mia could barely stand up she was so drunk. Or drugged. What if she'd needed to get rid of the thumb drive?

Her heart began to beat a little faster as she thought of Mia's condo. Was the thumb drive what the person had been looking for? She knew she was letting her imagination run wild and it wasn't like her.

Her earlier thoughts of Tag Cardwell as a cowboy spy was to blame, she told herself. And yet this could be the stuff of secret-agent novels. A spy who's been compromised and has to ditch the goods, an encrypted message and a mathematician who gets involved in solving the mystery.

And gets herself killed, she thought with wry humor.

But she couldn't help studying the letters. She knew a little about codes because they involved math and because she'd played around with them as a girl, sending "secret" coded messages to her friends about the boys she liked. Her friends struggled with the deciphering and tired of them quickly.

It had been years, but she remembered some of the basics. She began to play with the letters, noticing there were eighteen *W*s and sixteen *A*s.

The most common letters in the English language were *E, T* and *A*. So if these were English words, then *W* and *A* were probably one of those more frequently used letters. Though by the position of the *A* letters, they represented something other than *A,* she thought.

Her cell phone rang, making her jump. She was surprised to hear Tag's voice.

"I talked to my brother. He says the thumb drive didn't come from Ford."

"Really?" She was already pretty sure of that anyway, but she did like the sound of his voice. He had a wonderful Texas accent.

"I'm sure there's another explanation," he said.

She was, too.

"I'd better go. Just wanted to let you know." He seemed to hesitate.

She felt her heart beat kick up even against her will.

"Okay," he said.

"Thanks for letting me know. Maybe I'll talk to you later."

"Yeah."

She hung up, a little disappointed he hadn't asked her out—if that was what he'd been about to do earlier—but now all the more determined as she studied the letters again. Codes often involved simple addition or subtraction. She should be able to break this one by trial and error, but it would take time.

If it really was a code. She was glad she hadn't mentioned her suspicions to Tag, though. He thought she was geeky enough as it was.

TAG SWUNG BY his uncle's cabin. Who better to get the truth from than Harlan's brother? Tag had seen the look pass between them. He had a feeling there were few secrets between the two of them. If his father had a girlfriend, Angus would know.

But when he knocked at the door, there was no answer. He glanced in the curtainless window. The cabin was small, just three rooms, so he could see the bed. Clothes were thrown across it, the closet door open as if he'd packed in a hurry.

At the bar earlier, Angus hadn't mentioned going anywhere, especially this close to Christmas. Tag thought about the way the two of them had acted as they were leaving the bar. All his suspicions began to mushroom.

He checked the makeshift garage and found Angus's rig gone. Maybe he'd gone over to his daughter's. Tag drove on down the canyon to the Cardwell Ranch. This time Marshal Hud Savage was nowhere to be seen.

"I went by your dad's cabin," he said after Dana answered the door and ushered him into the kitchen, where she was baking cookies. The babies were napping, she said, and the two older kids, Mary and Hank, were with their aunt Stacy.

"It looks as if Angus is going out of town. I thought you might—"

"He's been called away on business," Dana said. "He wasn't sure when he'd get back, but he promised he would try his best to be here Christmas Eve."

"He got called away on business?" Tag couldn't help his skepticism or the suspicion in his tone. He couldn't imagine what business his uncle might have other than buying new guitar strings. "Just days before Christmas? What kind of business?"

She shot him a questioning look. "He's never said. Why?"

Tag let out a surprised sound. "So this isn't unusual?" Dana shook her head. "And you've never asked him?" He hadn't meant for his tone to sound so accusatory, but he couldn't help it. How could she not know what her father did for this so-called business?

"In case you haven't noticed, our fathers do their own thing. I'm not sure exactly what they do, but occasionally it takes them out of the canyon for a few days, usually on the spur of the moment."

This news came as a complete surprise. "Harlan does this, too? I didn't think either of them ever left. So they're *both* involved in this *business*?"

She gave him an impatient look, then shrugged.

"Aren't you suspicious?"

She chuckled. "*Suspicious?* Dad could have a whole other family somewhere. Maybe more than one. But if that's the case, he seems happy, so more power to him."

Tag couldn't believe her attitude. "Has either of them ever had girlfriends locally?"

She thought for a moment. "Not really. Maybe a long time ago. Like I said, they seem happy just doing their thing, whatever that is." She pulled a pan of cookies from the oven and deftly began sliding them onto a rack to cool.

As she did, she said, "Angus and I aren't that close. I'm busy with the kids and the ranch and Hud, and Dad's a loner, except for his brother...."

"I always thought that if I lived here, Harlan and I would be closer," Tag said as he took a seat at the table and watched her. He couldn't help feeling disappointed. He'd really thought this trip would bring him closer to his father. If anything, it seemed to be pushing them even further apart. "What is it about those two that they aren't good with their own kids?"

Dana sighed. "Or with their wives. They just aren't family men and never have been. But don't let that spoil your Christmas here," she said, and handed him a warm cookie. "We're going to have a wonderful time whether they make it Christmas Eve or not."

"Yes, we are," Tag said, sounding more upbeat than he felt. Right now, he felt as if the Grinch had already stolen Christmas.

After he left the ranch, he drove around aimlessly, hoping he might see his father or uncle coming out of one of the local businesses. Finally, he stopped for something to eat, but barely tasted the food in front of him.

When he came back out, he was surprised it was already getting dark. The sun had disappeared behind Lone Mountain several hours ago, and the deep, narrow canyon was shrouded in shadows. He'd forgotten how quickly it got dark this far north in the winter.

As he drove up to his father's cabin, he was relieved

to see Harlan's SUV parked out front. He'd half expected that, like Angus, Harlan had taken off for parts unknown on some "business" trip.

Wading through the snow and growing darkness toward the cabin, he was determined to get the truth out of his father. No more lies. Either that or he would have to go to the marshal with what he knew. Nix that. He'd have to take his suspicions to the cops in Bozeman, since he wasn't sure he could trust Hud. Admittedly, he didn't know much about Mia's death—or about his father's possible involvement. Just a gut feeling—and a leather jacket.

Deep shadows hunkered around the edge of the cabin as Tag started up the steps. He'd shoveled the steps and walk early this morning before he'd left to go Christmas tree hunting. That now seemed like a lifetime ago.

There had been some snow flurries during the day close to the mountains. The snow had covered the shoveled walk. Tag slowed as he noticed the footprints in the scant snowfall.

His father had had company. Several different boot prints had left tracks up the walk. One had to be his father's, but there were at least two others. His brother? But who else? He'd gotten the feeling his father had few visitors. Then again, he hadn't thought his father had female visitors and he'd been wrong about that.

Only one light shone inside the house. It poured out to splash across the crystal-white snow at the edge of the porch.

He slowed, listening for the sound of voices, hearing nothing. From the tracks in the snow, it appeared whoever had stopped by had left.

He thought of Dana now. Unlike her, he had to know what was going on with his father. He wasn't buying that they had "business" out of town occasionally. Monkey business, maybe.

As he opened the door and looked in, all the air rushed from his lungs. The cabin had been ransacked. He stared, too shocked to move for a moment. Who would have done something like this, and why?

He thought of the thick envelope that his father had given the marshal. Was that payoff money to keep a lid on what his father and uncle were involved in? The envelope had been thick. Where would his father get that kind of money? Not from playing his guitar at a bar on weekends.

Drugs? It was the first thing that came to mind. Were his father and uncle in the drug business?

At the sound of a groan, he rushed in through the debris to find his father lying on the floor behind the couch. Tag was shocked to see how badly Harlan had been beaten.

He hurriedly pulled out his cell phone and dialed 911.

Chapter Six

Hate is a strange but powerful emotion. Camilla went to bed with it each night; it warmed her like wrapping her fingers around a hot mug of coffee. It was her only comfort, locked away in this world of all-women criminals. The place didn't feel much like a prison, though, since it was right in the middle of the city of Billings.

Only when she heard the clang of steel doors did it hit home. She was never leaving here. At least not for a very long time.

Of course the nightmares had gotten worse—just as the doctor had said they would. She'd known they would since they'd been coming more often—even before she'd been caught and locked up. She'd wake up screaming. Not that screaming in the middle of the night was unusual here.

The nightmare was the same one that had haunted her since she was a girl. She was in a coffin. It was pitch-black. There was no air. She was trapped and, even though she'd screamed herself hoarse, no one had come to save her.

The doctor she'd seen a few years ago hadn't been encouraging, far from it. "Do night terrors run in your family?" he'd asked, studying her over the top of his glasses.

"I don't know. I never asked."

"How old did you say you were?"

She'd been in her late twenties at the time.

He'd frowned. "What about sleepwalking?"

"Sometimes I wake up in a strange place and I don't know how I've gotten there." But that could have described her whole life.

He'd nodded, his frown deepening as he'd tossed her file on his desk. "I'm going to give you a referral to a neurologist."

"You're saying there's something wrong with me?"

"Just a precaution. Sleepwalking and night terrors at your age are fairly uncommon and could be the result of a neurological disorder."

She'd laughed after she left his office. "He thinks I'm crazy." She'd been amused at the time. Back then she hadn't been sleepwalking or having the nightmare all that often.

Unfortunately that was no longer the case. Not that she worried about it all that much. So what if she got worse? It wasn't as though she was going anywhere, and everyone here already thought she was half-crazy.

So, Spark. How would you say you're dealing with prison life?

In her mind's eye, she smiled at her pretend interviewer. "I exercise, watch my diet and, oh, yes, I have Hate. It keeps me going. Hate and The Promise of Retribution, they're my cell mates."

Tell inquiring minds. Who's at the top of your hate list and why?

"It's embarrassing actually." Camilla thought about the first time she'd laid eyes on Marshal Hud Savage. The cowboy had come riding up on his horse. "Do you believe in love at first sight?" she asked her fictional interviewer. "Then I have a story for you."

"YOUR FATHER SAYS he didn't get a good look at the intruders," Marshal Hud Savage told Tag later that night at the hospital.

"How is that possible? They beat him up. He had to have *seen* them."

"What makes you think it was more than one man?" Hud asked.

"The tracks in the snow. There were three different boot prints. I'm assuming one pair was Harlan's."

Hud nodded. He seemed distracted.

Tag felt that same sick feeling he'd had earlier today when he witnessed his father with the marshal. "Harlan didn't mention anything when the two of you talked just after noon today?"

Hud frowned. "Why would Harlan—"

"You didn't see my father earlier today? I thought he said he was stopping by your place to talk to you."

The marshal's eyes narrowed before he slowly shook his head. "Harlan told you that? Maybe he changed his mind."

Hud had just lied to his face. "I must have misunderstood him." Tag felt sick to his stomach. What the hell was going on? "I hope you're planning to find who did this to him and why."

"I know my job," Hud snapped. "Look," he said, softening his tone. The marshal appeared tired, exhausted actually, as if he hadn't had much rest for quite a while. "When your father is conscious, maybe he'll remember more about his attackers."

It angered him that Hud was trying to placate him. "*If* he comes to." Harlan had fallen into a coma shortly after the EMTs had arrived to take him to the hospital. What if he didn't make it?

"Harlan's going to be all right," Hud said. "He's a tough old bird."

Tag hoped Hud was right about that. His cell phone rang. He checked it, surprised to see that the call was from Lily McCabe.

"Excuse me," he said, and stepped away to answer it. "Hey."

"I think it's in code." Lily sounded excited.

"Code?"

"The letters on that thumb drive, I think they're two lists of names."

"Names?" A call came over the hospital intercom for Dr. Allen to come to the nurses' station on the fourth floor, stat.

"I'm sorry. Did I catch you in the middle of something?"

"I'm at the hospital. Someone ransacked my father's cabin and beat him up."

"Is he all right?" She sounded as shocked as he felt right now.

"The doctor thinks he's going to recover. He's unconscious. The marshal is here now." He looked down the hall and saw that Hud was also on his cell phone. Tag wondered who was on the other end of the line. Uncle Angus?

"Did he tell you that Mia Duncan's condo was also ransacked?"

It took Tag a moment to realize she was referring to the marshal—not Harlan or Angus. "No, he didn't mention that." Another reason not to trust Hud—as if he needed more.

"That's odd. First Mia's condo is ransacked and she's

murdered, then your father's cabin and he gets beaten up. This is Montana. Things like that just don't happen."

Apparently they did. "That *is* odd," he said. First Mia's, now his father's place? Had Harlan come home and surprised his intruders? Or had they torn up the place *after* they tried to kill him?

"I'm sure there's no connection."

"Yeah." He didn't want to see a connection to his father and the murdered woman, but the coincidences just kept stacking up. "So you say those letters are actually names?" He knew he sounded skeptical.

"I have only started decoding them, but yes, they appear to be names. I can't really explain it over the phone. But I thought you'd want to know right away."

He glanced down the hall. Hud was still on his cell phone, his back turned to Tag. What if Mia had put that computer thumb drive in his pocket last night?

"I want to see what you've found." More than she could know.

"You're welcome to come up to my place when you're ready to leave the hospital."

"Give me your address. I'll come over as soon as I can, if that's all right."

She rattled off an address on Sky-High Road up on the mountain. "It's at the end of the road."

As he disconnected, he saw the doctor coming down the hall. "Harlan is conscious," he said to the marshal, then looked in Tag's direction. "He'd like to see his son."

Hud started to say something, but the doctor cut him off. "He said he'll talk to you after he talks to his son."

Tag walked down the hall and pushed open the door into his father's hospital room. Harlan looked as if he'd been hit by a bus, but he was sitting up a little and his gaze was intent as he watched Tag enter.

"You gave me a scare," Tag said as he stopped at the end of his father's bed.

"Sorry about that." Harlan's voice was hoarse. He was clearly in pain, but he was doing his best to hide it. "The marshal will catch the little hoodlums. How times have changed. They're targeting old people now for our prescription drugs." He chuckled even though it clearly hurt him to do so.

"Whoever beat you up, they weren't after your arthritis medicine," Tag said evenly. He couldn't believe how angry he was at his father for continuing to lie to him. "What were they really looking for, *Dad?*"

His father's expression hardened. "Stay out of this, son. That's why I wanted to see you. I want—"

"That woman who was at your cabin was Mia Duncan, wasn't it?"

Harlan sighed. "I told you. I don't know anyone by that name."

Tag shook his head and tried to still his growing anger. "You just keep lying to me. What business is Uncle Angus away on?"

"Why are you asking me that?"

"Because the two of you are inseparable. You can finish each other's sentences. You have to know where he's gone and why."

"I guess what I should have asked is why is it any of your business?" Harlan said, an edge to his voice.

Tag pulled off his Stetson and raked a hand through his hair as he tried to control his temper. "I know something's going on with the two of you, and it has to do with that woman who was murdered. Angus owns a snowmobile and he knows those old logging roads behind the ranch. You own snowmobiles yourself. I would imagine the two of you have been all over that country behind the ranch. Is it drugs? Is that the business you're in that gets your cabin torn up and you beat up and in the hospital?"

His father let out a sigh. "Do you realize what you're saying?"

"You lied to me. At the bar, I saw you watching the door. You were expecting Mia. You were shocked when I told you she was dead. That's why you didn't ask who was killed. Because you *knew*."

"This conversation is over." He reached for the buzzer to call the nurse.

Tag stepped to the side of the bed and caught his father's arm to stop him. "Tell me it isn't true. Tell me I've got it all wrong." He hated the pleading he heard in his voice.

His father met his gaze. "You have it all wrong."

"Then you don't mind if I keep digging into her death."

"Leave the investigating to the people who are trained for it. Please, son. I don't want to see you get hurt."

His father had already hurt him by not being in his life. But did he really believe Harlan Cardwell was… what? A drug dealer? Worse, a killer?

He met his father's steely gaze. "Then tell the truth."

"Stay out of this, Tag. It isn't what you think."

"I hope you're right—given what I'm thinking."

Harlan closed his eyes. "Tag, I need you to go back to Texas." When he opened them again, Tag saw a deep sadness there. "This isn't a good time for a visit. Please. Go home. Don't wait until after Christmas. If you don't—"

The door opened and the doctor came into the room. Harlan looked away.

"If I don't leave… What are you trying to tell me?" Tag demanded of his father. "That if I continue digging in your life I'll end up like that woman you don't know?"

"I'm sorry," the doctor said. "Did I interrupt something?"

"No. My son was just leaving," Harlan said. "Please don't tell your mother about this. I'll call you in a few days in Texas."

"Don't bother. I'll see you before then," Tag said, and left.

"YOU HAVE TO tell him the truth," Hud said after the doctor had left.

Harlan looked up at him from the hospital bed. "You know I can't do that." He motioned to the pitcher of water on the bedside table, and the marshal poured him a glass.

"He's your *son*," Hud persisted. "He isn't going to stop. That damned stubbornness seems to run in your family."

Harlan took a drink of water and handed back the empty glass. "I need you to persuade him to go back to Texas."

"I wouldn't count on that happening. He seems to know that you stopped by the ranch earlier today."

"How would he know that?" Harlan shifted in the bed and grimaced in pain.

Hud shook his head. "He knows and he's suspicious as hell of both of us."

"Have you heard anything from Angus?"

"Nothing yet."

"I tried to warn Mia…." Harlan looked away.

"She knew what she was getting into."

"I warned her what could happen if she got too close to the truth." Harlan turned back to him. "You didn't find anything?"

"Nothing. If she had it, then whoever killed her took it. Tag said she was drunk when he saw her at the bar."

"She had to be pretending to be drunk, maybe so she could leave early and not be stopped. Or maybe they got to her somehow." Harlan gently touched his bruised and swelling jaw. "We still don't know who was waiting for her outside the bar?"

"All Tag could tell us was that it appeared to be a dark-colored pickup and the driver was wearing a cowboy hat. I could take him in to look at mug shots."

Harlan quickly shook his head, then groaned in regret for doing it. "I need my son kept out of this. Do whatever you have to to make that happen."

"I can't very well arrest him without a reason to charge him."

Harlan closed his eyes. "You'll think of something. He seems hell-bent on finding out the truth. You know what's at stake. Stop him."

IT BEGAN TO snow as Tag left the hospital. He felt shaken as he slid behind the wheel of his rented SUV. What were his father and the marshal involved in? A cover-up regarding Mia Duncan's murder? Lily had said that Mia's condo had been ransacked. Clearly, whoever was behind this was looking for something.

He feared he knew what. Worse, that Lily had it.

As he watched large snowflakes drift down through the lights of the parking lot, Tag suddenly realized how late it was. But he couldn't stand the thought that Lily was in danger if that thumb drive was what the killers were looking for.

He started the SUV, still debating what to do because of the late hour and the snowstorm. Was it possible that Lily was right and Mia had put the thumb drive in his pocket? Why would she do that? Why give it to a complete stranger? Unless she knew she had to get rid of it quick?

With a start, he was reminded again of what she'd said.

"You look like him."

Had she known he was Harlan's son?

Tag shook his head. She'd been drunk or high on drugs. She hadn't known what she was saying. He thought of his father. He couldn't believe Harlan and Angus were drug dealers. And yet he didn't really know them. He especially didn't know his father, and the way things were going, he doubted he ever would.

His heart began to beat a little faster as he threw the SUV into Drive. Lily had the computer flash drive. If there was even a chance she was in danger... He drove by his father's cabin and got a pistol from Harlan's gun cabinet. He told himself he was just being paranoid.

As he headed toward Big Sky, he drove as fast as he could. He couldn't help being worried about Lily up in the mountains all by herself. He tried to assure himself that she was safe. No one knew she had the thumb drive.

His mind kept going back to last night in the bar and Mia, though. He remembered the way she'd clutched his jacket. She *could* have put the thumb drive in his pocket. Now she was dead. His father was in the hospital. And the killers were looking for something. It was too much of a coincidence that he'd found the thumb drive in his pocket. And now Lily thought she'd discovered the information on the computer USB was two lists of names in some kind of code?

Ahead, the road to the summit was a series of switchbacks that climbed from the river bottom to nearly the top of twelve-thousand-foot Lone Mountain. The snow fell harder the higher he drove. He had to slow down because of the limited visibility.

His mind was still whirling as he passed Big Sky Resort and left behind any signs of life. Up here, there was nothing but snowy darkness. He still couldn't get his mind around what was happening. His father was involved in whatever was going on, and so was the marshal, and he was betting his uncle Angus was, as well.

Harlan had said it was a bad time for a visit. No kidding. He was determined that Tag return to Texas. Hell, Harlan had almost threatened him, insinuating that if he stayed, it could be dangerous. Would be dangerous.

Heart racing, he reached into his pocket for his cell phone to call Lily. He had to make sure she was all right and to let her know he was almost to her house.

But as he started to place the call, he glanced in his rearview mirror, feeling a little paranoid. *You're not paranoid if someone is really after you,* he thought as he noticed a set of headlights behind him.

He watched them growing closer. The driver behind him was going too fast for the conditions and gaining on him too quickly. Tag looked around for a place to pull over, but there was only a solid snowplowed wall on one side of the road and a drop-off on the other.

Giving the SUV more gas, he sped up as he came out of a curve. Ahead was another curve. He could feel the glare of the headlights on his back, glancing off the rearview mirror and his side mirrors. The vehicle was almost directly behind him.

Tag told himself that the driver must be drunk or not paying attention or blinded by the falling snow. Unless the person behind the wheel was hoping to make him crash.

He tried to shake off even the thought. He wasn't that far from the road up to Lily's house. Suddenly the headlights behind him went out.

Glancing in his mirror again, he was shocked to find the vehicle gone. Had the driver run off the road? Or had he turned off? There had been a turnoff back there....

Ahead, Tag saw the sign. As he turned, he looked back down the main road. No sign of the other vehicle. Breathing a sigh of relief, he drove on up the narrow, snowy road. Wind whipped snow all around the SUV. He had his windshield wipers on high and they still couldn't keep up with the snow.

The road narrowed and rose. He knew he had to be getting close. He thought he caught the golden glow of lights in a house just up the mountain. His fear for Lily amplified at the thought of her alone in such an isolated place.

A dark-colored vehicle came out of the snowstorm on a road to his right. He swerved to miss it and felt the wheels drop over the side of the mountain, the SUV rolling onto its side. His head slammed into the side window. He felt blood run into his eye as the SUV rolled once more before crashing into a tree.

Chapter Seven

The snowstorm blew in with a fury. Inside the house, Lily could hear the flakes hitting the window. It sounded like the glass was being sandblasted.

She shivered and checked her watch as she went to put more logs on the fire. Tag said he would come as soon as he could. She told herself he'd probably been held up by the storm. She just hoped he would be able to get up the road.

Her house sat by itself on the side of the mountain, far from any others. The road often blew in with snow before the plows made their rounds. Since she didn't usually go to work at her brother's bar until the afternoon, it hadn't ever been a problem.

But tonight, she was anxious to show Tag what she'd come up with so far and she worried since there had already been some good-size drifts across the road when she'd looked out earlier.

She'd worked trying to decode the random letters until her head ached. What if she was wrong? What if this was nothing? But she was convinced that there were two lists of names. She'd gotten at least a start on the code, making her more assured that she was on the right track.

A loud noise from outside made her jump. She

stopped stoking the fire to listen for a moment and heard it again. Her pulse spiked before she could determine the sound.

She couldn't help being jumpy. Wasn't it enough that a woman she worked with had been murdered last night and another one was missing? But Lily didn't kid herself. Her nerves were more because of Tag and the thought of the two of them alone in her house.

Another noise, this one a loud thud. She peered out at the porch swing an instant before the wind blew it back into the side of the house again with a loud thump. The shadows had deepened on the porch, running a dark gray before turning black under the pines. The porch light illuminated only a small golden disk of light against the falling snow.

Hugging herself, she assured herself that there was nothing to be afraid of up here. She'd always felt safe. The porch swing thumped against the side of the house, followed by a loud thud closer to her front door. Probably that potted pine she had by the door. She started to turn back to her work when something caught her eye. Fresh footprints in the snow on the steps up to the porch.

A gust of wind blew snow against the glass. For a moment, it stuck, obstructing her view. Tag? Could he have come to the door and she hadn't heard him?

The knock at the door made her jump. She chastised herself as she hurried to the front door, thankful she'd been right and thankful, too, for Tag's company. Even for a short period of time tonight, she would be glad to have him around. Mia's murder must have her more shaken than she'd let herself admit.

As she turned the knob, the wind caught the door and wrenched it from her hand. It blew back on a gale, banging against the wall.

Blinded by the cold bite of the snow and wind, she blinked. Then blinked again in astonishment.

"Gerald?"

LILY HADN'T SEEN Gerald since the day before their wedding that had never happened because he hadn't shown up.

She stared at him now. Nothing could have surprised her more than to find him standing there, caked in snow and huddled into himself to block the wind.

"Would you mind if I came in?" he asked pointedly. "It's freezing out here."

She nodded, still too stunned to speak, and stepped back to let him enter, closing the door swiftly after him.

He brushed snow from his blond hair and slipped out of his wool dress coat, holding it at arm's length to keep the snow off him. He wore dark trousers, dress shoes and a white shirt, including a tie. The knot was a little crooked, which surprised her. Gerald valued preciseness in all things.

As he looked up at her, his blue eyes seemed to soften. She was struck by the memory of the two of them. Just last summer they'd been planning a life together. She remembered the smell of his aftershave, the feel of his fingers on her skin, the taste of his mouth when he kissed her. Like the wind outside, the force of his betrayal scattered those once pleasant memories, leaving her bereft.

She saw with a start that he was still holding his coat out as if waiting for her to take it. She finally found her voice. "Gerald, what are you doing here?"

The one thing she'd told herself she'd loved about this man was that he never wavered. Gerald exuded confidence. While she often felt swept along in his wake, she'd been happy to be part of his life even if it meant accepting that he knew best and always would.

"I had to see you," he said. He seemed to study her for a moment before he added, "I figured you'd be here. You look…tired."

She bristled at his words. Leave it to Gerald to speak the cold truth. He'd never been good at tempering his observations. "It's been a rough day. One of our servers was murdered."

"*Your* servers? You mean your brother's. You *are* still at the university, aren't you?"

"Yes." It annoyed her that he'd never understood why she spent the past few Christmas and New Year's holidays up here at Big Sky helping her brother. He'd always insinuated that Ace was using her and that serving cocktails was beneath her.

Gerald must have seen that he'd irritated her because he softened his tone and asked, "How *is* James?"

"Fine." There was no reason to pretend any further that Gerald cared about her brother. He had always refused to call him anything but James, saying that Ace was something you might call a dog.

"You said you had to see me," she reminded him.

He was still holding his coat away from him as he looked behind her into the living room. "Is there any chance we could sit down and discuss this like rational evolved human beings?" There was an edge to his words as if he'd expected her to be more gracious.

She thought how he hadn't shown up at the wedding. The pain and hurt had dulled over the past six months, but there was still that breath-stealing reminder when she thought of her humiliation.

She'd hadn't been heartbroken—not the way she would have been had she and Gerald shared a more passionate relationship.

"We're cerebral," Gerald used to say. "It's a higher level of intimacy than simple passion. Who else could appreciate you the way I do?"

"And who else could love such a math nerd," his sister had said, "but another math nerd?" That, too, Lily had believed was true. So what if they didn't have a passionate relationship? They had math.

She thought of Tag and his comment, *"You counted them?"* He'd thought she was joking. Probably hoped she was joking.

But Gerald had embarrassed and hurt her and left her feeling as if no one would want her if he didn't. Now, though, he was back. What did that mean?

"Yes, please sit down." She took his coat and hung it up, feeling conflicted. She wanted to throw him out and yet she wanted, needed, to hear what he had to say.

Leaning toward throwing him out, she reminded herself that Gerald had understood her in a way no other man had and he had come all this way to talk to her. And while they hadn't been the perfect couple in some aspects, they had a lot in common, since Gerald had been the head of the math department. That was until he took a job in California without telling her.

"Can I get you something to drink? I have a wine you might like," she said, using the manners boarding schools had instilled in her.

He shook his head as he tested the couch with his hand, then sat down. She'd forgotten he did that. He tested things, weighing them as to how worthy they were, she'd always thought. For a long while, she'd thought that was why he hadn't shown up at the wedding. She just hadn't met his high level of quality.

"Please sit," he said, looking up at her still looming over him. "You're giving me a crick in my neck."

She sat across from him and immediately wished she'd gotten herself a glass of wine. Also, her instant response to his command annoyed her. She almost got back up just to show him he couldn't come into her house and start telling her what to do after what he'd done to her.

"I'm sorry," he said, stilling her in her chair.

Those were two words she'd never heard from him before. She waited for more.

"I can't explain my actions."

And still she waited.

"I deeply regret what I did." Gerald had always been a man of few words as if they cost him each time he spoke and he refused to waste a single one.

A gust of wind rattled the window behind her, making her turn. All she could see was blowing snow and darkness beyond the arc of the porch light.

"Are you expecting someone?" Gerald demanded, clearly annoyed that her attention had wavered.

She thought of Tag. He apparently wasn't coming. "No. No one." Lily had barely gotten the words out of her mouth when there was pounding at the door. She jumped up in surprise. So did Gerald.

"I thought you weren't expecting anyone," he said suspiciously.

She said nothing as she hurried to the front door. As she opened it, a gust of wind and snow whipped in, but she hardly noticed.

"What happened to you?" she cried when she saw Tag standing there, his face covered in blood.

"SOMEONE RAN ME off the road," Tag said as she ushered him into the house. "Do you still have the—" The words *thumb drive* died on his lips as he saw the man standing behind her.

"We need to get you to the hospital," she cried.

"No," he said, his gaze still on the man standing in Lily's living room. "I'll be all right."

"Then at least let me clean up that cut over your eye. I'll get the first-aid kit." As she hurried past the man toward the back of the house, she said over her shoulder, "This is Gerald." Lily disappeared into a back room, leaving Tag alone with the man.

A brittle silence fell between them until the man said, "I don't believe I caught your name, but you're bleeding on her floor."

"Here," Lily said, hurrying back into the room with the first-aid kit, a washcloth and a towel. She shot Gerald a warning look as she passed him. "His name is Tag. Tag Cardwell."

"Tag?" The man said it and grimaced. "Charming."

Lily seemed to ignore him. "Sit down here and let me see about that cut. Are you hurt anywhere else?"

Tag grimaced as he lowered himself into the chair she pulled out. "Just beat up and bruised. My ribs hurt, but they don't feel broken. Everything else seems to be working since I was able to walk the rest of the way up here." He grimaced again as the washcloth touched the cut on his temple.

"Sorry," she said, and reached into her pocket. "Here, take two of these. The prescription is a recent one of mine from a sprained ankle I had." She jumped up to hurry to the kitchen for a glass of water.

He took the pills and the glass of water she handed him. He tossed the pills into his mouth and downed them with the water. His gaze met hers as he handed back the empty glass. "Thanks."

"What is this about you being run off the road?" Lily asked.

Now that he was here, Tag was questioning what exactly *had* happened. He'd been so anxious to get to Lily and make sure she was safe… "Just some driver who wasn't used to Montana weather." At least he hoped that was all it had been. The driver had kept going, though, hadn't even stopped to see if he was all right. But if he really was drunk, then he wouldn't want to be involved.

Gerald cleared his throat. "I should probably go since you're obviously busy," he said as he walked over to the table. His fingers ran along the top of the open laptop computer sitting there.

"Please don't touch that," Lily said, and got up to go to the table. She closed the computer and pulled out the thumb drive, dropping it into her sweater pocket before returning to Tag. Picking up the washcloth, she began to bathe his face.

"I can do that," Tag said, and took the cloth from her, smiling at her tenderness. He wiped away the dried and frozen blood he could feel on his face before she took the washcloth back and dabbed at a couple of places he'd apparently missed.

"It seems I'm not the only one anxious to talk to you tonight, although I didn't make as dramatic an entrance as your…friend," Gerald said, plainly irritated. Tag wondered what he had interrupted.

"If you're staying in the area, Gerald, perhaps we could talk tomorrow," she said without looking at the man as she gently dabbed at the area around Tag's cut before reaching for the antiseptic.

"What choice do I have if I hope to get this settled?" Gerald snapped.

"I thought it *was* settled," she said, anger sparking just under the surface. Tag liked the heat he saw in her eyes and thought about the first night they'd met. A woman with attitude, his favorite kind, he thought as he felt the pain pills start to work.

"This is definitely not what I'd hoped for," Gerald said with a sigh. "I will call you tomorrow if you think you can make time for me."

"Fine."

Tag wondered what was unsettled between them, but was smart enough not to ask. Yep, the pills were definitely working. They were strong, which was fine with him. He hurt all over and was thankful when the pain began to numb.

"I'm sorry if I interrupted something," Tag said as the door shut behind Gerald. "It sounded as if he really wanted to talk to you tonight. I didn't mean to run off your boyfriend." Yep, the pills were working. He felt drunk with them. Whatever they were, they were *very* strong.

"He isn't my boyfriend," she said as she put a bandage on over his cut. "He's my former fiancé."

"You were going to marry that jackass?" The words slipped out before he could stop them. "Sorry."

"I'm afraid you witnessed Gerald at his worst," she said as she finished bandaging his wound.

Tag was trying to imagine Gerald at his best. "So, why didn't you marry him?"

"There," she said, and closed the first-aid kit. "He stood me up at the wedding."

"The bastard. If I'd have known that, I would have slugged him for you."

She met his gaze and began to laugh. "That's what my brother always threatened to do."

"Why didn't he?"

"Gerald left town. This is the first time I've seen him since the day before the wedding."

"And you didn't hit him the moment you saw him?"

She shook her head. "I'm a perfectly reasonable woman. I don't hit people."

"I would have hit him."

She rose to put away the first-aid kit, but stopped. "Are you all right?"

He realized he'd been staring at her, wondering how some goofy older guy like Gerald had gotten a beautiful young woman like Lily to even look twice at him. "Fine. What were those pills anyway?"

"I think I'd better drive you to the hospital or at least down to the clinic. Just let me put this away—"

He caught her arm. "I'd rather hear about this code you told me about."

"I think it's a list of names. I'm still decoding them. If Gerald hadn't shown up when he did…" She glanced toward the door and he saw pain in her expression.

The man had hurt her. Tag really wished he'd slugged him. Was it possible he'd been driving the car that had run him off the road? "He didn't give you any indication why he came up here tonight?"

She shook her head.

"Because I interrupted the two of you. I'm sorry."

"Don't be. I'm not sure there is anything he could say under the circumstances." Her smile was filled with sadness.

"Look, he's bound to have realized what a fool he was. He probably came here tonight to beg you to take him back. Maybe you should call him and—"

"Six months ago, he left me at a church filled with our relatives and friends on our wedding day. Apparently he didn't have anything to say that day. I'm sure whatever he plans to say now can wait a day."

If Tag had been up to it, he would have gone after Gerald and kicked his sorry butt. He couldn't believe it had taken the man six months to come back. "I'm sorry he hurt you like that," he said, taking her free hand. She didn't pull away. "Are you sure you want to take him back? You deserve a lot better." He caressed the back of her hand with his thumb pad. Her skin was so warm and smooth.

His gaze went to her mouth. It was a Cupid's bow, as kissable as any mouth he'd ever seen. "Lily—"

"I really should drive you down to the clinic to make sure you don't have any internal injuries," she said.

"You're not driving anywhere in this storm. I hope Gerald is staying on the mountain and not planning to drive all the way to Meadow Village tonight." Lily said nothing. Nor did she draw her hand back. "I'm afraid we're snowed in," he said, lulled by the pain pills she'd given him and this woman.

"I should show you the code I worked out so far on the data from the thumb drive," she said, and started to pull away, but he drew her back. "Or should we call the marshal first? You really should report the accident."

"Do you still love him?" Tag asked as he got to his feet and, taking the first-aid kit, put it aside. He felt a little woozy.

"Gerald?" she asked. "I don't know. You should sit back down. You're hurt."

"Tell me you haven't been waiting around for the past six months for him to come back." He saw the answer in her eyes and swore.

"Tag." His name on her lips was his undoing. Outside, the storm raged. Inside, he threw caution to the wind as he drew Lily to him.

Chapter Eight

Tag woke naked and smiling. Without opening his eyes, he felt across the bed for Lily, remembering last night and their lovemaking. Finding the bed empty and cold, he opened one eye. No Lily.

He couldn't help being disappointed. Last night had been amazing. He hadn't expected that kind of passion in her, he thought as he touched his shoulder and felt scratches. He chuckled to himself. She'd been wild, surprising herself as well as him, he thought. But there had also been tenderness. Lily McCabe was all woman, as sexy as any he'd ever known.

"Lily?" No answer. His heart kicked up a beat. She wouldn't have tried to leave this morning on her own? Or worse.

Swinging his legs over the side of the bed, he was reminded of the wreck and the aching parts of his body. He managed to pull on his jeans before hurrying barefoot out to the kitchen. He was met with the welcoming scent of coffee and the sight of Lily standing silhouetted against the bright clear morning.

"Hey," he said, relief in his voice. He'd planned to come up behind her, wrap his arms around her and kiss her on her neck, then do his best to persuade her to come back to bed with him.

But she turned too quickly, separating them with more than the cup of coffee in her hand. He stopped short and felt his heart drop. This was not the wild woman he remembered from bed last night. Her expression warned him to keep his distance.

He blinked, confused. Last night had happened, right? He thought of their lovemaking. Was it possible he'd only dreamed making crazy, passionate love with this woman last night?

Lily's demeanor told him it had only been a figment of his drug-induced imagination and if he wasn't careful, he would make a fool out of himself. It wouldn't be the first time. Or the last, he thought. He had to know.

"Uh, did something happen between us last night?"

"Happen?" She took a sip of her coffee, watching him over the rim of her cup. Her hair was still damp from her shower, smelling of jasmine—just as it had last night in his arms. But she was looking at him as if he was crazy.

He remembered how strong the pain pills had been. Sure, he'd felt groggy, but— "I woke up naked this morning and I thought I remembered you and me..." The look she gave him stopped him from being more specific.

"Do I seem like the kind of woman who would fall into bed with a man I hardly know?"

He studied her, considering her words. She wore a turtleneck sweater and jeans. Buttoned up, that was how he would have described her. Nothing like the woman last night.

"No, you don't. But last night—" Last night he remembered finding a side of Lily that was as unexpected as the way she was acting this morning. "Sorry. It's just that I..." He shook his head and warned himself not to get in any deeper.

"I think you really should see what I found on the thumb drive," she said, all business, as she moved to the table where she'd left her laptop and the papers she'd been working on.

He was suddenly more aware of the fact that his body hurt all over and his head felt as if it was filled with lint. He stood looking after her, unable to accept that last night had been nothing more than a dream. He remembered every kiss, every touch. Desire stirred in him.

"Tag?" Lily glanced back at him, her gaze taking in his bare chest. "Perhaps you'd like to get dressed first."

"Yeah." He touched his scratched shoulder. Was it possible he'd gotten that in the accident? He met her gaze and for just a moment—

She quickly looked away, busying herself with the calculations she'd made. "We can discuss this when you come back. I'll pour you a cup of coffee. How do you take it?"

"Black and strong." He realized he needed his wits about him. Not only for whatever was going on with his father and this thumb drive, but with this woman.

LILY WATCHED TAG walk to the bedroom and closed her eyes as she fought the images. She couldn't believe what had happened last night. That hadn't been her, she told herself just as she'd told Tag.

All morning, she'd fretted about what they would say to each other once he woke up. She'd never been like that in her life.

But when she'd realized that he hadn't remembered...

"You took the coward's way out," she whispered to herself, and felt her face heat with embarrassment. Better than the desire that had burned through her veins at the sight of him this morning dressed only in jeans.

She was just glad he didn't remember. What had possessed her to fall into the cowboy's arms last night? Lily didn't delude herself. Seeing Gerald again had thrown her into a tailspin. She'd felt all the hurt and betrayal and a part of her had wanted to forget—and possibly even the score.

Lily laid her head on her arms on the table. She knew it had been a lot more than just escape or getting even with Gerald. She'd *wanted* Tag. Wanted him in a way she hadn't even been able to imagine. He was everything Gerald wasn't. She'd known instinctively that their lovemaking would be nothing like what she'd known with her former fiancé.

"Boy howdy," she said, repeating an expression she'd picked up from Tag. As she heard Tag come out of the bedroom, she lifted her head and pushed away those embarrassing thoughts. She hated lying to him. Fortunately Tag had remembered just enough with the pills she'd given him to think he'd dreamed their wanton night of passion. Best leave it that way since it was never happening again.

The thought gave her a dull ache at her center.

What made her angry with herself aside from lying to Tag was that she felt as if she'd cheated on Gerald. She knew that made no sense. She owed him nothing— less than nothing. But she also knew that he wouldn't have come all the way from California and driven up to her house in a blizzard last night if he wasn't planning on asking her to take him back.

She told herself that she and Gerald belonged together. They were perfect for each other. Both math nerds, they had their careers in common. Last night had just been one of those crazy things that never happened to a woman like her.

Lily convinced herself that she would put it behind her. Gerald was her future. She would forgive him and they would get married—just as it was meant to be.

She quickly straightened as Tag came into the room. But she kept her eyes on the computer screen even though she'd memorized the letters there since she'd looked at them so many times. Remembering she'd said she would pour Tag a cup of coffee, she jumped up and bumped into the edge of the table.

Her coffee sloshed over onto some of the papers. She lunged for them and, off balance, stumbled into Tag— the very last thing she wanted to do.

"Easy," Tag said as he caught her.

"I was going to get your coffee," Lily said, more nervous than he'd ever seen her.

"I can get my own coffee. Are you all right?" Holding her like this, he could feel her soft, full curves. He recognized every one of them, he thought with a start. His imagination was great, but not this good. Something had happened last night. But why would she lie?

Because you let her think you couldn't remember, you damned fool.

She pulled away as if realizing he was remembering last night. Or was he still deluding himself? She turned her back to him as she poured his coffee. He could see that her hands were shaking.

Tag wanted to call her on her lie, but when she turned back to him, he saw the glow in her cheeks. Could she be embarrassed about last night? She'd definitely let her hair down, so to speak. How innocent *was* this woman? Surely there were other men besides dull Gerald.

"Thank you," he said as he took the coffee cup she offered him. Lily was clearly rattled. Maybe she regretted last night and really was embarrassed.

What was it she had said? "Do I seem like the kind of woman who would fall into bed with a man I hardly know?"

"So, what's this about a code?" he asked, and took a sip of his coffee. He saw Lily's instant relief as she hurriedly sat back down at the computer. He could see where she had been writing a series of numbers and letters on scratch paper.

"After I came back here, I began to play with the letters. I know they appear to be random, but I don't think they are," she said, eyes bright. She clearly loved this stuff. "They appear to be part of a code. Julius Caesar invented one like it nearly two thousand years ago. He was invading countries to increase the size of the Roman Empire and he needed a way to communicate his battle plans with his generals without the enemy finding out by intercepting his messages."

"How do you know all this?" Tag asked, even more intrigued by this woman.

"It's math. Simple addition or subtraction, actually. Caesar, instead of writing the letter *A,* would write the letter that comes three places further in the alphabet, the letter *D.* When he got to the end of the alphabet, he would go right back to the beginning so instead of an *X,* he would write an *A.* You get the idea."

He did, but he wondered how the devil she'd figured that out and said as much.

"The more I studied the letters, the more they didn't appear random at all. The spaces made me think they were a list of names."

"Written in code?"

She nodded, her eyes bright. She was in her element. He wondered if he would ever see all the different sides of Lily McCabe. "A version of Caesar shift."

"And you can read what it says?"

"Not completely yet. It's a case of trial and error with only twenty-five different possible shifts before you can see a pattern. Caesar shifted the alphabet forward three spaces. This code is tougher, but in the end it will come down to simple mathematics."

He couldn't help smiling at her passion. He had a flash of her in his arms, naked, her skin silken and scented with jasmine, her mouth wet as she dropped it to his. Tag shook himself, the image so real he almost kissed her.

She didn't seem to notice. She was studying the letters on the page and her scribbles again. "Though I would have thought someone who didn't want the code deciphered would have used symbols instead of letters," she said, bending over one of the papers. "That way there could be four-hundred-billion possible combinations instead of only twenty-five. Not that it couldn't be broken by frequency analysis, though. Mary, Queen of Scots, used symbols for her code when plotting against Elizabeth the First. It got her beheaded."

Lily stopped talking and looked up at him, her gaze locking with his. "Your eyes haven't glazed over," she said, sounding surprised.

"This is fascinating. I'm amazed. How did you figure it out?"

"I'm using the frequency analysis method. Since *E, T* and *A* are the most frequently used letters in the English alphabet and there are eighteen *W*s and sixteen *A*s…The *A*s are not really *A*s, you understand. Once you have the most-used letters, it is just a matter of figuring out the rest of them."

He watched her bite her lower lip in thought.

"I can't help thinking whoever made up the code is a novice at this," she said. "They probably went online, typed in codes and thought 'here's one.' The problem is they must have written this in a hurry because they made mistakes, which is making it harder for me to decode."

Nothing about what she was doing looked simple to him. Just staring at the letters made his headache worse.

"I should be able to break it soon," she assured him.

"Lily, I have a bad feeling that the reason Mia's condo was ransacked and my father's, too, was that they were looking for this thumb drive."

"Then you should take it to the marshal," she said, handing it to him. "I have a copy of the letters on my computer, so I can keep working on the code."

He nodded, although he had no intention of taking it to the marshal. Not until he knew which side of the fence Hud Savage was on.

"Until we know what's really on this," he said, "I wouldn't mention it to anyone, all right?"

She nodded.

"I need to get to the hospital and see my father, but I don't like leaving you here snowed in alone."

She waved him off. "The plows should be along in the next hour or so if you want to take my SUV."

He wasn't about to leave her here without a vehicle even if he thought he could bust through the drifts. "Are those your brother's cross-country skis and boots by the door? If you don't mind me borrowing them, I'll ski down to the road and hitch a ride. My brothers and I used to do that all the time when we were kids."

"If you're sure…." She turned back to the papers on the table. "I'll keep working on the code and let you know when I get it finished."

She sounded as if she would be glad when he left her at it. He was reminded that she also had plans to talk to her former fiancé today. He felt a hard knot form in his stomach. Jealousy? Hell, yes.

Except he had nothing to be jealous about, right? Last night hadn't happened. At least that was the way Lily wanted it. He fought the urge to touch her hair, remembering the feel of it between his fingers.

"I want you to have this." He held out the pistol he'd taken from his father's. "I need to know that you are safe."

She shook her head and pulled back. "I don't like guns."

"All you have to do is point it and shoot."

Lily held up both hands. "I don't want it. I could never…" She shook her head again.

"Just in case," Tag said as he laid it on the table, telling himself that if someone broke into her house and tried to hurt her, she would get over her fear of guns quickly. At least he hoped that was true.

LILY STOOD AT the window, watching Tag cross-country ski down the snowed-in road until he disappeared from sight. He glided through the new snow with no wasted movement. She could practically see the muscles rippling in his arms and back.

At the memory of the feel of those muscles, she shivered and stepped away from the window, cradling her mug of hot coffee to chase away the chill. Why had she lied to him about last night?

It wasn't a lie. She wasn't the kind of woman to

fall into a stranger's arms. Nor did she recognize that woman who'd made such passionate love to Tag last night.

What had she been thinking? She was still shaken. True, she'd been thrown completely off balance by finding Gerald at her door.

In her heart of hearts, she'd dreamed of him coming back, begging her to forgive him. She'd just expected it to happen a lot sooner. That *was* what he wanted to talk to her about, wasn't it? He wanted her back. He'd realized what a colossal mistake he'd made. That was what it had to be. Gerald was safe, and right now she wanted safe, didn't she?

What would have happened if Tag hadn't shown up when he had? Would she have let Gerald stay? Would they have made love as they'd done in the past? Or would they have had a wild, passionate night as she had with Tag?

Wasn't that what she'd always wanted?

As hard as she tried, she couldn't imagine Gerald ever being like that.

But their relationship was built on intellect and a shared passion for math, she reminded herself.

She closed her eyes, images of her lovemaking with Tag making her go weak in the knees. She quickly opened her eyes. She'd never get the code finished if she kept letting her mind stray.

And yet as she headed for the computer again, she couldn't deny the ache low in her belly. She wanted Tag again.

That was why she had to see Gerald. She needed to put an end to these thoughts. All last night had been was one wild fling before she took Gerald back.

And if Tag had remembered last night?

Lily sighed and glanced toward the open bedroom door and the rumpled sheets. The two of them would be in that bed right now.

She blew out a sigh that lifted her drying bangs from her forehead. Her skin felt oversensitive as if Tag's touch was branded on it. She hugged herself for a moment, remembering how wonderful he'd been. She worried though that he was in trouble because of the thumb drive.

Determined to figure out the code, she had started back toward the table and her laptop when she saw the gun. Stepping to it, she gingerly picked it up with two fingers, then wasn't sure what to do with it.

One of the drawers in the kitchen was still open from where she'd gotten a clean dish towel out this morning. She walked over to it and dropped the gun into the drawer and closed it. She wouldn't need it. Even if she did, she knew she could never fire it.

She had started back to work on the code when the phone rang not ten minutes later. The sound irritably jerked her out of her calculations. She saw it was Gerald and almost didn't answer.

ONCE TAG REACHED the main road, he easily caught a ride to his father's cabin. The day was bright, sunny and beautiful, so there was a lot of traffic coming and going on the road to the ski hills.

At his father's cabin, he called the rental company about the wrecked SUV. The cabin was still a mess, but the crime-scene tape had been removed. He changed clothes and headed for the two-car log garage next to the cabin, anxious to get to the hospital and see his father.

But when the garage door moaned open, he saw something that stopped him dead. His father's SUV was gone. With a start, he remembered that the SUV had been parked outside yesterday when he'd found his father had been attacked.

He tried to tell himself that a friend must have borrowed it as he climbed into Harlan's old pickup. The key was in the ignition. Harlan always left his keys in his rigs as if daring someone to steal them. Maybe that was what had happened, although he feared there was an even simpler explanation.

When he reached the hospital and walked into his father's room, Tag wasn't surprised to find the bed empty.

"Are you looking for Mr. Cardwell?" a nurse asked as he let the door close with a curse.

"Yes. Has he been moved to another room?" He knew he was only deluding himself.

"I'm sorry, but he checked himself out."

"Against doctor's orders, right?"

The nurse smiled and nodded. "He is a very stubborn man."

"Isn't he?" Stubborn and hiding something. Tag hated to think what.

There were only two other places he could think of to look for his father. He tried his cousin Dana's first.

Tag found her and her two oldest kids putting the finishing touches on the worst-looking Christmas tree he'd ever seen.

"Do. Not. Say. A. Word," she warned him, and grinned. "This tree needed a Christmas."

"It needs limbs and needles," Tag said. "Jingle Bells" played on the radio in the kitchen, and he thought he smelled ginger cookies baking. For a moment, he wanted to help string the paper garland the children had made and curl up in front of the fire. This was the

Christmas he'd envisioned. Not one involving lies and murder.

"It's one of Mama's orphan trees," six-year-old Hank said. "It made Daddy laugh."

"But it made Mama cry," the younger Mary said.

"Tears of joy," Dana hurriedly added, and smoothed a hand over Mary's dark hair so like her mother's. "Want to join in the fun?"

"Thanks, but I need to find my father. You haven't seen him, by any chance, have you?"

Dana shook her head. "I did hear that he checked himself out of the hospital. I'm sure he's fine."

Tag wasn't so sure about that. "You haven't heard from Angus, have you?"

"Grandpa is away on business," Hank said, making his mother smile.

"I thought I'd check his favorite bar...." He could see that Dana wasn't going to be of any help. Because she didn't understand her father any better than he did his, she'd taken a "whatever" attitude. He wished he could.

ACE LOOKED UP when Lily walked into the bar. "What's wrong?"

Where did she begin? "Someone ran Tag off the road last night on the way to my place. He could have been killed. He played it down, but I think it has something to do with the thumb drive he found."

"Tag?" Her brother grinned. "On the way to your place? I thought there was a rosy glow to your cheeks."

If he only knew. "That's all you got out of what I just told you?" She shook her head. "Gerald showed up at my place last night."

That got his attention and wiped away Ace's cat-who-ate-the-canary grin—just as she knew it would. "What did that bastard want?"

"I'm pretty sure he wants me back."

"What?" Ace demanded. "I hope you told him where he could stick—"

"Tag interrupted whatever Gerald was going to say. I'm on my way to meet Gerald now."

"You're actually thinking of going back to him."

Her brother had a way of seeing through her that annoyed Lily to no end. "Gerald and I have—"

"So help me, if you take that lily-livered son of a b—"

"It's my life, Ace."

He shook his head. "Exactly. You want to spend it with a stiff shirt like Gerald? Or a man like Tag Cardwell?"

She wanted to point out that neither Tag nor any other man like him had asked, but changed the subject. "Did you hear what I said about someone running Tag off the road last night?"

Ace nodded. "Does he think it was an accident?"

"He pretended it was."

Her brother rubbed his jaw. "Teresa hasn't turned up yet, and with Mia murdered… I just don't understand it. This is usually such a safe place."

She glanced at her watch.

"Don't do it, Lily."

She looked at her brother, confused for a moment.

"I know you. You're going to end up feeling guilty for not taking him back—after *he* deserted you on your wedding day." He shook his head again. "Why aren't you mad? You should be spitting nails. He doesn't deserve you."

She nodded, thinking Tag had pretty much said the

same thing. "I have to go. Are you opening the bar tonight?"

"Got to. If Teresa isn't back, I'm going to need you to work."

"Don't worry. I'll be here."

"Lily?"

She had started to leave, but now she turned back to look at her brother. Even frowning, he was drop-dead gorgeous. Why hadn't some woman snatched him up? Or was he like her? Always playing it safe, afraid to really let go and fall for someone who made him see fireworks on a freezing winter night just before Christmas.

Ace shook head as if changing his mind about whatever he had been going to say. "Just be careful, okay?"

She had to smile. Too bad he hadn't been around last night to warn her. It was a little too late now. "Always levelheaded. That's me. And, Ace, don't mention the thumb drive to anyone, okay?"

Chapter Nine

It had been weeks in this prison and Camilla was growing all the more impatient. She was wondering what she was going to have to do to make Edna's acquaintance, when one of the woman's minions brought her a note.

She had to think outside the box to decipher the misspelled words, but then again not everyone in prison had a master's degree. Hers was in psychology. Basically, a con man's dream curriculum. No wonder she was so good at reading people.

Except for Hud Savage. You certainly read him wrong, didn't you, Miss Smarty-Pants?

Her mother's voice. She ground her teeth. That "misstep" had cost her dearly. Which was why retribution had such a nice ring to it. *You know retribution, don't you, Mother?*

The note from Edna wasn't a request, but a command appearance, making her think about telling the inmate standing in front of her what she could do with her missive. The woman, a skinny former addict with a tattoo of a rattlesnake around her right wrist, was known as Snakebite. The nickname probably had more to do with her disposition, though, than the tattoo.

Feeling in a generous mood and needing to get her plan moving, she merely smiled and said, "Okay."

"Now, bitch."

Camilla considered kicking the woman's butt, convinced she could take her.

Snakebite had the good sense to take a step back as Camilla got to her feet.

Edna was waiting for them in the craft area of the prison. A kind-looking woman with a huge bosom and small delicate hands, she looked as if she should be in a kitchen baking chocolate-chip cookies for her grandkids. Which could explain her nickname, Grams.

"I heard you've been asking around about me," Grams said, and motioned to the chair across the small table from her. Snakebite took a position next to the wall along with another of Edna's "girls," a large woman called Moose.

"I heard you were the kind of woman who got things done."

Grams lifted an eyebrow.

Camilla leaned in closer. "I didn't get a chance to tidy up before I got sent here."

Grams smiled. "So you're a neat freak?"

She laughed and leaned back. "I guess I am."

"It isn't cheap cleaning up messes."

Camilla smiled. She had money stashed around the country under a dozen different names and she had ways to get to it. "I didn't think it would be."

"How do I know I can trust you?" Grams asked.

"The same way I know I can trust you. Otherwise how would either of us be able to sleep at night?"

The older woman laughed again and slid a pen and paper across the table.

Camilla wrote "Marshal Hud Savage" on the slip of paper and slid it back across along with the pen.

Grams raised a brow again.

"Is there a problem?" Camilla asked.

"Not a problem exactly. I'm just curious. Is this personal or business?"

"I wouldn't think you would care. It's personal," Camilla said, remembering the way Hud had rebuked her. "It's *very* personal."

Grams shrugged and tucked the piece of paper into her bra. "I'll get back to you."

"How long before it's done?"

"Patience," she said as she pushed herself to her feet. "Time is relative in here. But I think you'll be pleased." With that, Grams padded off, her "girls" behind her.

Camilla picked up a lump of clay from a tub left on the table and began twisting it in her hands. First Hud. Then she would take care of the rest of his precious family. As Grams said, she had nothing but time.

WHEN GERALD OPENED his motel room door, Lily took a step back.

"Don't look so surprised to see me," he said irritably. "You act as if you expected me to leave town before you arrived."

When he'd called, he'd sounded…odd. Hurt, no doubt because she hadn't fallen into his arms instantly. Hadn't forgiven him without hesitation. That she'd been more concerned with Tag than him last night.

"Truthfully, Gerald, I don't know what to expect from you," she said as he moved aside so she could step in out of the cold. She took in the room. Gerald had always been excessively neat. The bed was made, his suitcase perfectly packed and open on the luggage rack by the wall.

"I told you I needed to talk to you," he said behind her, a slight whine in his voice.

She turned to look at him. "But you didn't say why."

"I didn't get a chance before your...friend showed up. Lily, I hate to see you get involved with someone like him."

"I beg your pardon?"

"That cowboy. What could you possibly have in common with him?"

If he only knew. "That's none of your business."

Gerald let out a snort. "You can't be falling for a man like that."

She started to deny that she was falling for Tag but stopped herself. "I can fall for anyone I want to."

"Lily," he said impatiently.

"Gerald," she said, matching his tone.

His eyes narrowed.

"Gerald, just tell me what it is you want."

He let out a long sigh. "I had hoped we could sit down and discuss this reasonably like intelligent adults, but if you insist..." He met her gaze. "I shouldn't have done what I did."

"No, you shouldn't have. Is that all?"

"No," he snapped. "I told you about my little sister who lives in California."

Lily frowned. "She works for a bank."

"An investment company," he said, and looked away. "She got into some trouble. I had to...help her." His gaze met hers. "I didn't want to hurt you, but I really had no choice. She's my little sister. That's why I took the job in California, why I've done everything that I have."

"You had a choice, Gerald. You could have told me about your sister, you could have told me you didn't want to get married *before* the wedding. Don't tell me you didn't have a choice."

"You are making this very difficult, Lily."

"Oh, I'm sorry, Gerald." He usually didn't get sarcasm, but she had laid it on so thick, even he got it.

He had the decency to look chastised. "I'm sure it was also difficult for you."

"Difficult, Gerald? You mean when I had to explain to our friends and family why you left me standing at the altar when I didn't have the *slightest* idea?" she demanded, surprised at her anger. Even more surprised that she was letting it out. Gerald had always felt such a show of emotions distasteful at best. In her, he'd seen any emotional display as a sign of immaturity. Since he was eleven years her senior, she'd locked up all her emotions so as not to seem childish.

But now she thought of Tag and her brother, both filled with righteous indignation over what Gerald had done to her and demanding to know why she wasn't furious. Because she had every right. Just as she had every right to let her anger come out now.

"I apologized for that," Gerald said evenly.

"Six months later," she pointed out. "Not that I have any more idea now than I did then why you would do such a rude, disrespectful, embarrassing, ob—"

"I couldn't go through with it right then. My sister needed me and I...I panicked, all right?"

She raised a brow. "*You* panicked?"

"You have to know how hard this is to admit. I found myself in a position where I had to make a decision.... I should have told you."

"You think?" Speaking of childish.

He narrowed his eyes as he studied her. "I knew you'd be upset, but I had hoped you wouldn't be bitter."

She almost laughed.

"You seem so…different."

She *did* laugh. "You know, Gerald, being stood up at the altar changes a person."

He seemed not to know what to say.

Lily hadn't thought she'd changed from the woman who'd agreed to marry the head of the math department at the university, but she realized she had. She was stronger, just as her brother had said. She'd gotten over the initial pain and realized that she'd survived one of the most awful things that could happen to a woman.

Last night when she'd seen Gerald, all those old initial feelings had come back in a rush. Followed quickly by the hurt and betrayal.

Since then, she'd let herself admit that she *was* angry. No, she was furious with him and all the more furious with herself because she'd actually thought about taking him back. She'd actually wanted that ordered life he'd promised.

But standing here with him now, she knew that her night with Tag had changed all that. She'd never loved Gerald the way a woman should love a man she was about to marry. Tag had shown her what she'd been missing. Passion. And now that she'd experienced it, she could never go back to that lukewarm idea of love she'd shared with Gerald.

Nor had Gerald loved her enough to be honest with her. Plus, as Tag had said, Gerald was a coward for not facing her on their wedding day.

"Was there something else?" she asked her former fiancé, feeling the weight of the past lift from her shoulders.

Gerald looked confused. He'd obviously come to her thinking all he had to do was tell her he was sorry and that he wanted her back. He seemed more than a little astonished that that hadn't been the case.

"I guess there is nothing else to say. I made the decision to help my sister. If it matters, you're making that decision easier."

"I'm all about making your life easier, Gerald," she said.

"I didn't mean to make you angry again," he added quickly. "You know I tend to speak sometimes without considering how it affects others."

She started for the door.

"I couldn't help noticing when I was at your house that you were working on something," he said. "Is it something I can help you with?"

Lily turned to look at him. "That's nice of you, but—"

"I would like to help you. I'd feel better about the way I'm leaving things between us," he said.

She felt herself weaken. She'd been interrupted so much she hadn't been able to work on decoding the data she'd taken off the thumb drive. If Tag was right and this information was important in Mia's murder case... "I *could* use your help."

He looked pleased as well as curious as she dug in her bag and pulled out the papers she'd been working on. She set them on the desk, spreading them out as she explained what she'd come up with so far.

"It would be easier if I had the original," he said, glancing at the papers.

"I don't have it with me."

He nodded, pulled up a chair and, taking one of his pens from his pocket protector, began to check her work—just as he had done when he was her teacher.

Lily watched him. She'd known how easily he could

be distracted with a puzzle involving math. The mathematician in her still loved that about him.

"Interesting," he said as he bent over the letters.

GUHA BKOPAR
CAKNCA IKKNA
BNWJG IKKJAU
HSQ SWUJA
YHAPA NWJZ
NWU AIANU

LWQH XNKSJ
IEW ZQJYWJ
YWH BNWJGHEJ
HWNO HWJZANO
DWNHWJ YWNZSAHH
DQZ OWRWCA

She'd decoded enough to see a pattern, but it hadn't held up either because whoever had come up with the code had been in a hurry and made mistakes or because they'd gotten confused and sloppy.

As she watched Gerald work, she saw that she'd been right. There were two lists of names. It amazed her how quickly he filled in the names. She had to give him credit. Gerald really was a master at this sort of thing.

"You were on the right track," he said. "Just off a little." Within minutes, he'd come up with two lists of names. "Is this all?" he asked, sounding disappointed as he handed the sheets to her and rose from the chair. "You're sure there was nothing more on the original data?" He obviously would have much preferred some cryptic message. She would have, as well.

She glanced at the names, one of them taking her breath away.

Gerald didn't seem to notice as he walked over and closed his suitcase with a finality that rang through the room. But when he turned toward her again, he said, "You and I are good together, Lily. You need me, now maybe more than you realize. I should leave you my cell phone number in case you change your—"

"I won't change my mind, Gerald," she said as she shoved the papers into her shoulder bag with trembling fingers.

"I see." He had pulled out his business card as if about to write his new cell phone number on it, but now he stuck it back into his pocket. "I hope you don't live to regret this, Lily. Clearly your behavior has taken a dangerous trajectory—if that cowboy is any indication."

She smiled. She'd never been one to hold grudges, always quick to forgive and forget. But she took some satisfaction in realizing that Gerald was jealous. If he only knew…. "Goodbye, Gerald."

He started to reach for her as if to kiss her cheek as he used to do when they parted, but she stepped back and walked out the door, leaving him standing there.

She had a death grip on her shoulder bag and the papers inside, and couldn't wait to show Tag. As she walked out, she heard Gerald's cell phone ring.

"Yes, I talked to her," he said into the phone. "No, she won't listen to reason."

Gerald had apparently involved one of his sisters, Lily thought as she rushed to her vehicle. *No, she won't listen to reason?* She gritted her teeth, never more glad that she hadn't weakened and gone back to the man.

She was so deep in her thoughts that she didn't even notice the large black SUV parked next to her on the driver's side. Nor did she hear the back door of the SUV open or the man jump out directly behind her.

Lily didn't even have time to scream as something wet and awful smelling was clamped over her mouth and she was dragged into the black pit of darkness in the back of the massive SUV.

Chapter Ten

Hud got the call on his way from the hospital. He'd gone by to see Harlan Cardwell only to find that the man had left without anyone having seen him leave.

The marshal listened to the news on the other end of the line with the same sinking feeling he'd had earlier. Another young woman's body had been found.

"I'll be right there," he said, hung up and turned on his flashing lights and siren. If he could have gotten his hands on Harlan Cardwell right now...

Last night at the hospital he'd demanded to know more than the information he'd been given yesterday at the ranch.

"We think it's possible Mia passed information to someone when she knew she was in trouble," Harlan told him. "She and Teresa Evans were apparently friends. Teresa would be the most likely person to give the data to if she was in trouble, which could explain Teresa's disappearance."

Hud had shaken his head in frustration.

"I wish I had an answer for you. They tried to kill me earlier. If Tag hadn't come along when he did ..."

"Aren't you getting too old for this?"

Harlan had chuckled even though it must have hurt him. "I only got involved again because of Mia." His voice broke. He cleared his throat. "I just talked to the coroner a few minutes before you came in. Mia had been drugged. We can only assume one of the patrons at the bar stuck her. She must have realized it too late to get the item to me. I'm sure she did everything she could to finish her mission."

"If Mia gave whatever this information is to Teresa Evans, then they have it."

Harlan shook his head. "Apparently Teresa didn't have it. They're still looking for it. At least that's what I'm hearing."

"How many more are they going to kill to get it?" Hud had demanded, and seen the answer in Harlan's eyes.

So the call that a young woman had been found on the ice at the edge of the Gallatin River hadn't come as a surprise—just another blow. Hud felt helpless for the second time in his life. The other time, just months ago, was when he realized a psychopath had his wife and children.

TAG GLANCED AT his watch and then tried Lily's cell phone again. It went straight to voice mail just as it had done the three times he'd tried before. He didn't leave a message.

He'd been trying since he'd gotten her cryptic message.

"Tag, the list is decoded. There's a name on here... you need to see. Call me. It's urgent."

When Lily had mentioned that she thought the thumb drive had two lists of names on it, he'd thought of his father. Was his father's name on it?

Tag thought of the ransacked cabin. His hand went to his pocket. He closed his fingers over the small computer flash drive. He'd thought taking it would protect Lily. But now she'd decoded it and had found a name. A name that had put her in danger?

Earlier he'd driven down to the Corral Bar, but the bartender said he hadn't seen Angus or Harlan since yesterday. He didn't seem that surprised, which Tag took to mean both men disappeared occasionally.

It baffled him as he drove back toward Big Sky.

Like a lot of Montana winter days, this one was blinding with brilliance. The sun hung in a cloudless robin's-egg-blue sky and now shone on the fresh-fallen snow, turning it into a carpet of prisms.

As he pulled up in front of the Canyon Bar and climbed out, he sucked in a lungful of the freezing air. Nearby pines scented the frosty breeze. He didn't see Lily's car, but he figured her brother would have heard from her by now. The fresh snow creaked beneath his boot soles as he crossed to the bar.

The front door was open even though the bar wasn't scheduled to open for another hour. As the door closed on the bright winter day behind him, Tag stopped just inside to let his eyes adjust to the semidarkness.

"We don't open for another…" Ace's words died off as he looked up from behind the bar. "Tag, come on in. I forgot to relock the door after Lily left."

"So you've seen her today?" Tag asked as he walked over to the bar.

Ace's expression changed into one of mild amusement. "She looked better than I'd seen her looking in a long time."

"Then she told you about Gerald."

"Gerald didn't put those roses in her cheeks," he said with a laugh. "What can I get you to drink?"

"Nothing, but thanks. I was looking for Lily."

"Like I said, she was by earlier. Gerald called her. She went to see him." Ace stopped in midmotion, a bar glass half-washed in his hand. "You met Gerald, right?"

"Last night."

"Then you know he's all wrong for her."

Tag didn't feel he could weigh in on that.

"I hate it, but she went to hear him out," Ace said with a disgusted shake of his head. "I was hoping we'd seen the last of him. I'm afraid she'll go back to him. Maybe already has."

That would explain why Lily wasn't answering her phone. "Maybe I will have that drink, after all," Tag said, and took a stool. "Just a draft beer."

Ace laughed and reached for a clean glass as the bar door opened again and a large silhouette filled it.

HUD PARKED AT the edge of the fishing access road a few hundred yards from the river and walked. His head ached, his stomach felt oily. It took all his mental strength not to stop and throw up in the fresh snow at the edge of the road.

He could see the flashing lights ahead. The coroner had been called. Second time in two days. Another dead young woman.

The body lay on the edge of the thick aquamarine-blue ice in a bed of snow. At first glance it appeared the woman had lain down in the snow to make a snow angel. Her arms were spread wide, facedown, legs also splayed. He'd guess she'd been thrown there and that was how she'd landed. Which meant she'd been dead before she hit because she hadn't made a snow angel. She hadn't moved.

"What do we have?" Hud asked the coroner after giving a nod to his new deputy, a man by the name of Jake Thorton. He'd come highly recommended but hadn't been tested yet. Nor had Hud made a point of getting to know the man. Jake seemed to keep to himself, which was just fine with his boss.

"Looks like strangulation," the coroner said. "Maybe that combined with hypothermia. Won't know until the autopsy. But she didn't die here."

Hud nodded. "Do we have an ID?"

"Found her purse in the snow over there," Deputy Thorton said. "Her name, according to her Montana driver's license and photo, is Teresa Marie Evans, the missing woman last seen at the Canyon Bar."

Teresa had a winter scarf tied too tightly around her neck—just like Mia. "Tire tracks?" Hud asked Jake.

"The road hadn't been plowed. Didn't look as if any vehicles had been down it. But there were tracks. I saw that she was dropped by snowmobile," he said. "I took photos."

Hud nodded at the young handsome deputy, thankful he was on the case since his own mind was whirling. All his self-doubts seemed to surface in light of another death. Dropped by snowmobile just like the last one.

"I'll let you handle this, notify the family, do what has to be done," he told Jake, and looked at his watch. Police officer Paul Brown's funeral was in two hours. Hud wasn't sure how much more death he could take.

AS THE MAN stepped into the Canyon Bar, the door closing behind him, Tag saw that it was Gerald, Lily's former fiancé. Or should he say now current fiancé? Had Lily gone back to him?

He waited almost expectantly for Gerald to approach the bar. The beer he'd downed turned sour in his stomach as he braced himself for the news. Like her brother,

Ace, Tag thought this man was all wrong for the woman he'd made love to last night. He reminded himself that Lily had regretted their lovemaking. Had that alone driven her back into this man's arms?

"Lily left this," Gerald said, and dropped a torn sheet of paper on the bar.

Tag's first thought was that she'd left a note for her brother.

"What am I supposed to do with this?" Ace asked after giving it a cursory glance and tossing it back on the bar.

"I wonder why I wasted my time," Gerald said with a shake of his head, and turned to leave.

Tag shifted on the stool to see what was on the sheet of paper. He recognized Lily's neat script. His pulse took off like a rocket when he saw the familiar array of letters from the thumb drive.

He quickly picked up the partial sheet of paper. It had been torn. Only a few of the original letters from the thumb drive were on the sheet. Next to them were other letters that made…*names*.

He didn't recognize any of them and frowned. Lily had been upset on the phone. *"Tag, the list is decoded. There's a name on here…you need to see. Call me. It's urgent."*

She'd wanted him to see a name, but it wasn't on this portion of the original sheet of paper.

"Wait a minute," he called to Gerald's retreating back. "Where's Lily?"

Gerald stopped, impatience in his stance, and then turned with a sigh. "You're asking *me?*"

"*You're* the one she went to see," Ace interjected.

Lily had solved the code. Whatever name had upset

her wasn't on this sheet. Tag slid off his stool and moved quickly to Gerald. "*Where's* Lily?"

Gerald gave him a smug, satisfied smile. "The last time I saw her she was leaving my motel room."

"Did you see where she went from there?"

He looked angry. "If you must know, I wasn't paying any attention."

Tag turned back to the bar and Ace. "Lily's message earlier said it was urgent I see these names, but I don't recognize any of them. Where are the rest of them?"

"What does it matter?" Gerald asked sarcastically but he stepped back toward the bar.

"Trust me, it might be a matter of life or death."

"Don't tell me she's in trouble because of what is written on that paper," Ace said as he leaned across the bar to take the scrap of paper in Tag's hand.

"Lily was convinced these letters had something to do with Mia Duncan's murder."

Ace let out a curse.

"That list of names?" Gerald asked. "*Murder?* This was exactly what I feared when Lily insisted on working in a...bar."

"Gerald," Ace said in clear warning. "Don't make me come over this counter and punch you." He turned to Tag. "What do we do?"

"If Lily's right, then I know who I need to talk to," Tag said. "If things go badly, though, can I depend on you to bail me out of jail?"

"I'm going with you," Ace said only seconds before a bunch of skiers came through the door and headed for an empty table. "I'll close the bar and—"

"No. Lily might come back here. Or you might be contacted. Anyway, you can't get me out of jail if you're in there with me." Tag scribbled his cell phone number on a bar napkin. "Call me if you hear anything."

Ace nodded as another group of patrons came through the bar door. Reggie showed up then in jeans and the Canyon Bar T-shirt, like the one Lily had been wearing the first night Tag met her. The night he'd also met Mia Duncan.

"I suppose you're both going to just assume I would be of no help?" Gerald asked.

"Call the bar if you hear from Lily," Tag told him, thinking Lily might contact Gerald before either him or her brother. "Ace will pass along the message." He started for the door.

"That scrap of paper in your hand. That has only some of the names on the lists Lily showed me," Gerald said. "I can't imagine how it could matter, but I'm the one who helped her decode them. If you have the thumb drive…"

Tag stopped at the door and turned. His hand went to the thumb drive in his pocket. "How do you know about that?"

Gerald rolled his eyes. "How do you think? Lily asked me to help her finish decoding the names."

So it was like that, Tag thought. Lily wouldn't have told him about the thumb drive or asked him unless she trusted him, unless she had gone back to him.

"Ace, can we borrow your computer?" Tag asked, and led the way to Ace's office.

Gerald sat down behind the desk, then held out his hand. Tag dropped the thumb drive into it and sat as Gerald went to work. It didn't take him long. When he finished, he printed out a sheet with the names on them and handed both it and the thumb drive back to him.

Two lists of names, just as Lily had suspected. The

names began to jump off the page at him. This was why Lily had wanted him to see them.

Mia Duncan's name was high on the list.

Not far under it was the name Harlan Cardwell. Directly under that was Marshal Hud Savage.

KYLE FOSTER
GEORGE MOORE
FRANK MOONEY
LOU WAYNE
CLETE RAND
RAY EMERY

PAUL BROWN
MIA DUNCAN
CAL FRANKLIN
LARS LANDERS
HARLAN CARDWELL
HUD SAVAGE

What the hell is this? He had no idea, but he was all the more worried about Lily. "You're sure you don't know where Lily went after she left your motel room?" he asked Gerald.

"I thought she must have left with you."

"Why would you think that?"

"Because she left her SUV in the parking lot."

"What parking lot?" Tag demanded, feeling his heart slamming against his rib cage. The names on the list. While he had no idea what they meant, he had a terrible feeling that they had gotten Mia Duncan killed, his father beaten to within an inch of his life and both Mia's and his father's homes ransacked. And now Lily appeared to be missing.

"The Happy Trails Motel down the highway," Gerald said.

Tag headed for the door at a run, praying he was wrong and that there was an explanation other than the one that had him terrified.

"I'll drive up to her house and check there," Gerald said to his retreating back. "You better not get her killed, Texas cowboy."

Tag didn't have time to go back and slug the suit or he would have.

The drive to the motel, although only half a mile, seemed to take forever.

He was in sight of it when he heard the news report on the radio. He hadn't even realized the radio was on, droning in the background, until he heard the announcement come on.

"A woman's body has been found along the Gallatin River two miles south of Big Sky. The name of the victim is being withheld pending notification of family. If anyone has any information, please call the marshal's office…."

An eighties song came on the radio.

Not Lily. No, it couldn't be Lily.

Ahead, he saw Lily's SUV parked off by itself. His stomach dropped. As he jumped out, he could see where another vehicle had pulled in next to it. And in the snow that the plow had left, he could see that there'd been a struggle.

Lily's boot-heel prints had made a short trail from her SUV driver's-side door to whatever had been parked next to it.

Chapter Eleven

As Tag drove straight to the marshal's office, he kept remembering the marshal and his father, heads together, arguing about something before his father gave Hud an envelope. Money? A bribe? A payoff?

Whatever it was, it had something to do with Mia Duncan—and if he wasn't wrong, the damned thumb drive in his pocket and the names on it.

He didn't know his cousin Dana's husband. This trip to Montana had been the first time they'd met. Was it possible Hud was crooked?

Tag hoped not for his cousin's sake. But look how she'd turned a blind eye to whatever Harlan and Angus did when they left the canyon. Would she be the same way if her husband were on the take?

All Tag knew was that he didn't trust the marshal. But right now he needed to know who had been found near the river. He glanced at the list again, surprised by the one name that seemed to be missing. Teresa Evans. How did she fit into all this? Or did she? He'd heard that she was missing. Was it her body that was found by the river?

He had to know.

Just as he had to know why both his father's and Hud's names were on the list. He had no idea what to make of that. Or how this list from the thumb drive could have anything to do with what was going on. Why would anyone be ransacking residences at Big Sky, let alone killing people for it?

All he could assume was that the names were important. *Why else had Mia put the thumb drive in his pocket?* he wondered as he stormed into the marshal's department and demanded to see Marshal Hud Savage. How important? He was about to find out since Hud Savage's name was on one of the lists.

"He's gone to a funeral," a pretty, redheaded young woman told him.

That threw him. "Whose funeral?"

"Officer Paul Brown."

The name was like a lightbulb coming on in his face. Paul Brown. He was also on the list.

"I just heard on the radio about a woman's body being found by the river." He held his breath. "Tell me it isn't Lily McCabe."

The woman dispatcher frowned. "Lily? No. But I can't give you—"

Not Lily. He felt his heart rate drop some. Not Lily. Not yet. "Where is the funeral?"

The dispatcher hesitated.

"I wouldn't ask but it's urgent," Tag said. "Another woman has disappeared."

"By now they would be heading for the graveside. Sunset. It's between Bozeman and Belgrade on the old highway. If you hurry—"

But Tag was already out the door.

LILY WOKE TO darkness, dying of thirst. Her mouth felt as if it had been stuffed with cotton balls. She tried to swallow as she sat up and blinked at the blackness around her.

At first she'd thought she was in the bedroom and Tag was beside her. But in a flash, the earlier events came back with the terror of her abduction.

Panic overtook her like a blizzard. Where was she? Her hand touched something cold and she recoiled. As her eyes became more adjusted to the dark, though, she saw that it was only a water bottle.

She snatched it up and drank half of it before a thought surfaced that made her quickly pull it away from her lips.

What if it was drugged? Or poisoned? Or all the water she had for however long she was going to be trapped here?

She didn't kid herself that she could climb off this mattress and walk out of here. The edges of the room began to take shape as her eyes adjusted to the darkness. Knotty-pine walls, dark with age, a linoleum floor. No apparent windows. One door. She could make out a tiny strip of light around its frame.

A basement, she thought, in some older house or cabin. Probably a cabin, which might mean she was still in Big Sky.

She considered yelling for help only an instant before she heard heavy footfalls coming down what sounded like stairs above her.

Lily thought about getting up, hating to be at such a disadvantage on the bed, but when she tried, she found she was too weak to stand. Sliding on the mattress until her back was against the wall, she stared in the direction of the single door in and out of the room. She told herself that the person wasn't coming to kill her or he would have already done that, but she knew killers probably weren't logical.

Whoever was outside the door put down something on the floor. It made a shadow under the door. Then she heard the key being turned in the lock. The door swung open along with blinding light before a large figure filled the doorway.

STANDING AT THE edge of the graveside service, Marshal Hud Savage tightened his grip on his hat held at his side as he saw Tag Cardwell pull up and get out of his father's old pickup.

Hud was in no mood for trouble and yet one look at the young man's face and Hud knew that was what was heading for him. He stepped a few feet back from the others. "Not here," he said under his breath as Tag reached him.

"Here or you come with me now," Tag said quietly under his breath. "Your choice. Unless you want everyone here to know about you."

Hud gave him a sidelong glance. "I could have you arrested—"

"I have what you've all been looking for. Set up a trade for Lily. *Now.*"

That got Hud's attention. He turned and headed toward the old pickup Tag had arrived in. Once there, he turned on the man. "What the hell are you talking about?"

"Lily McCabe. I know you have her and if you hurt her—"

"Tag, I don't know what you're talking about. Is Lily missing?"

"I'm tired of playing games with you and my father and uncle," Tag said, and swore.

Hud listened as Tag told him about seeing the leather jacket on his father's couch, catching his father in a lie, seeing Hud and Harlan the day Mia Duncan's body turned up.

"You've got it all wrong," Hud said when Tag finished.

"Yeah, that's what my father keeps telling me. Where is he, by the way?"

Behind them, Hud heard the graveside funeral procession breaking up. "We can't talk about this here. What was that that part about a thumb drive?"

Tag smiled. "So you did hear me. Make the call. As soon as I see Lily—"

"I can see how you might think I'm involved in all this—"

"We don't have time to—"

"I'm telling you the truth. Show me what you have. Maybe between the two of us we can—"

"So help me, if you have touched a hair on her head—" Tag swore, and grabbed Hud by the throat. A minute later he was being pulled off the marshal by two other law enforcement officers who'd been at the funeral. A minute after that he was in handcuffs in the back of Marshal Hud Savage's patrol SUV on his way to jail.

"You're being cheated."

The raspy words entered Camilla's right ear, the hoarse whisper sending a chill down her spine. She was standing in the prison chow line, not that she was hungry. She ate because food kept her strong. If she ever had a chance of getting out of here, one way or the other, she needed to keep up her strength.

"Don't turn around."

She fought the urge.

"She shouldn't be charging you." She could feel the woman's breath on her neck, hot and damp and putrid.

Camilla waited. Prison was teaching her patience and she'd become an astute student since she hadn't killed anyone yet.

"Just nod your head if I'm right." The woman moved closer. Camilla had to steel herself not to shudder. "You're paying Grams for a hit on a cowboy cop, right?"

Just like in high school, rumors ran rampant. This one just happened to be true.

She gave a short nod and could no longer contain the shudder.

The woman behind gave a snort. "His name was already on the list."

Camilla turned in her surprise to find Snakebite behind her. Their eyes met, Snakebite's as hard as obsidian. She turned back around as the line moved and felt sick to her stomach. Not because Grams had planned to charge her *and* someone else for the same hit. But that Marshal Hud Savage was about to be killed and it wouldn't be her doing.

She wanted to howl out her pain and yet she couldn't even step out of line. She shuffled forward, the smell of some awful casserole filling her nostrils and making her even more nauseated.

I have to get out of here.

Not just out of the line, but out of the damned prison.

I have to get out of here.

Camilla hadn't realized she'd said the words aloud. Not until she heard the raspy voice answer.

"I thought you might say that."

MARSHAL HUD SAVAGE pulled off onto a narrow snowy road that ended at the river's edge.

"You should take off my handcuffs," Tag said from the back of the patrol SUV. "Might look more believable that I made a run for it when you kill me."

Hud cut the engine and turned to look at him in surprise. "You think I'm going to kill you?" He let out a curse and shook his head. For months he'd been telling himself he'd lost his edge. That he wasn't any good at this anymore. He'd never felt more assured of that than at this moment.

"I'm not a dirty cop," he said, feeling himself hit bottom. "Why would you think—"

Tag snorted. "I saw my father give you an envelope the morning Mia Duncan was found murdered. Tell me that envelope wasn't filled with money."

"It wasn't." He thought of the paperwork Harlan had finally turned over to him. The agency was always holding out on him. With a shock, he had just been told that he had a dead agent on his hands and Harlan had still wanted to keep secrets. They'd argued until Harlan had finally given him some information.

"Look, I don't care, all right?" Tag said. "I just want to find Lily."

"So do I. That's why you have to help me with what you know."

"You expect me to trust you after all the lies you've told me? I know my father was seeing Mia Duncan."

"You have it all wrong."

"So you all keep telling me," Tag snapped.

Hud took off his Stetson and raked a hand through his hair. "I don't know how you managed to get so deep in all this." He met Tag's gaze. "I pleaded with Harlan to tell you the truth, but he didn't want you involved."

With a sigh, he said, "Mia was an agent. Your father was working with her."

"An agent?" Tag let out a laugh. "And my father was working with her? What would Harlan—"

"Harlan and Angus are retired, but they often help when needed."

Tag shook his head in obvious disbelief. "You're telling me my father and uncle are…agents?"

Hud nodded. "They've always worked undercover operations because they had such perfect covers with their band. Apparently Mia was getting close to busting a murder ring."

"Murder ring?" he said, sounding disbelieving.

"We're wasting time. You want to find Lily, you have to tell me about these names you said she had." He could tell that Tag didn't believe him. "You have to trust me if want to find Lily."

"Take off my handcuffs. If I can trust you, then trust me."

He hesitated. Tag was a loose cannon. He'd gotten involved and now Lily McCabe was missing. Hud already had two dead women. He hoped he wasn't making another mistake.

"I know you don't trust me, but I have reason not to trust you, either," Hud said as he got out of the patrol SUV and opened the back door. "You show up just before Mia is killed and we only have your word that she left with some Montana cowboy in a pickup."

"You can't be serious. Take off my handcuffs. I think I have what everyone is looking for."

Hud lifted an eyebrow, then unlocked the cuffs and watched Tag rub his wrists. He'd taken a chance with one of Dana's so-called cousins and almost gotten his family killed. And here he was again, taking another chance, one that could get him killed, as well.

TAG'S HEAD WAS whirling. He still wasn't sure he believed Hud, let alone trusted him. But right now he needed all the help he could get finding Lily.

"I have a partial list of some names that came off a thumb drive that I now believe Mia Duncan put in my coat pocket the night she was murdered." He dug out the scrap of paper with only a few of the names and handed it to the marshal.

Hud stared down at it, his eyes widening.

"You recognize the names?"

"Two of them are men who were recently released from prison," the marshal said as he turned the scrap of paper over, no doubt looking for more names. "One of them is dead. The other one, Ray Emery, is from around here. I don't recognize the others. Where is the rest of this sheet?"

Tag felt his heart hammering in his chest. He hoped he wasn't making a mistake that would get Lily killed—not to mention himself. He reached in his pocket and handed Hud the complete list from the thumb drive that Gerald had provided.

KYLE FOSTER
GEORGE MOORE
FRANK MOONEY
LOU WAYNE
CLETE RAND
RAY EMERY

PAUL BROWN
MIA DUNCAN

CAL FRANKLIN
LARS LANDERS
HARLAN CARDWELL
HUD SAVAGE

He heard the air rush from the marshal's lips and watched him swallow.

"This is the murder list," he said. "You say Mia put this in your coat pocket at the bar that night? Those names." He pointed to the ones on the top. "Those are the killers."

"And the names on the bottom?" Tag asked, his heart in his throat.

"Those are the hits."

"My father's name is on that list."

Hud nodded. "So is mine."

"How many of them are already dead?"

"Two that I know of. Paul and Mia. But Cal and Lars could already be dead by now."

"Then my father might be next." He met the marshal's gaze and let out a curse as he had a terrible thought. "You don't think they took Lily, not for the list, but…"

"As bait to flush out your father. Harlan said if you hadn't come by his cabin when you did, he would be dead. They wanted the thumb drive, but they didn't want him dead until they had the list that incriminated every prisoner who'd been released."

"I don't get why it's so important."

"In order to get released prisoners to kill for them, they had to promise their anonymity. If word got out that the feds had gotten hold of one of the lists…"

All Tag could think about was the fact that his father's name was on the list and the ones above might already be dead.

"Where is Harlan now?" When Hud hesitated, Tag said, "It's too late to hold out on me now."

"I honestly don't know. Apparently Mia had been working with a prison snitch. She'd heard that several prisons had started a type of co-op. For a fee, you can have someone on the outside killed. A recently released inmate kills someone he doesn't know, has no connection to. In return he gets either money or a favor. The idea is that the former inmate won't get caught because he has no motive."

Tag got it. His heart pounded as he realized why they were so desperate to get the thumb drive. "This list links the hits with the former inmates." This was incriminating stuff that could shut down the murder ring.

"I know Lily knew Mia and was the one who discovered her condo had been ransacked, but why do you think her disappearing has anything to do with the murder list?" Hud asked.

"Lily was with me when I found the thumb drive in my pocket. Once she took a look at what was on it, she determined it was written in some kind of code."

Hud frowned. "How did they know she had the thumb drive—let alone that she'd decoded it?"

Tag felt his heart drop. "I don't know. I thought she and I were the only ones who knew about it."

As THE MAN entered the room, Lily was blinded by the sudden light for a moment. He carried a tray and she caught the smell of a microwave dinner. Her stomach growled. She was surprised that she was starved. It seemed odd to her to think about food at a time like this.

Her gaze went from the tray to the man. He was big

and bulky with hamlike hands and arms covered with tattoos. Over his head, he wore one of those rubber Halloween masks, this one of an ogre.

She didn't miss the irony as she watched him put down the tray on the end of the mattress. She thought about jumping up and making a break for the door. Or grabbing the tray and attempting to hit him with it.

But even if she hadn't felt so weak from whatever they'd knocked her out with, she knew either attempt at escape would be wasted effort. Better to eat the food he'd brought, get her strength back and bide her time.

He didn't say a word as he turned and walked out of the room. Nor did he appear to be worried about a surprise attack from behind.

She thought she probably should have tried to make conversation with him. Hadn't she heard somewhere that in a situation like this you needed to make yourself as human as possible to your abductor?

But Lily was smart enough to know that this wasn't a garden-variety abduction. The fact that they hadn't killed her outright probably meant they were holding her hostage.

Just as she surmised that this had to have something to do with the thumb drive and Mia's murder—as she and Tag had guessed.

The thought of Tag brought tears to her eyes. Why hadn't she admitted that they'd made love? They would have been in her bedroom at the house in each other's arms—instead of her being here.

She'd let fear keep her from him. But she'd never seen herself the way she was with Tag last night. Nor had she ever felt as close to another human being. She ached for Tag Cardwell, and that scared her, too, because she feared Gerald was right and Tag was all wrong for her. A mathematician and a Texas cowboy? Their lives were miles apart in more than distance.

And yet she couldn't get him out of her racing heart. She tried not to let herself think about what would happen if these men didn't get what they wanted as she dragged the tray over to her and dug into the food. It was as wonderful as it was awful. She thought of Gerald and his contempt for any food that wasn't four-star-restaurant quality.

She actually smiled at the absurdity of it all since she practically licked the cardboard container clean. The food made her feel a little stronger. But what boosted her more than anything was the knowledge that Tag would be looking for her.

Lily hugged herself, thinking about last night and their lovemaking. He was the kind of man who would ride in on a big white horse and save her. A sob escaped her lips. What if he hadn't gotten her message? Or worse, what if these men had already found Tag and taken care of him?

She assured herself that the cowboy wouldn't let her die without a fight.

Chapter Twelve

Everything could be bought for a price. Camilla had learned that at an early age. That price though was often very high—and too often wasn't monetary. So she'd spent her life paying dearly.

Because of that, it didn't come as a surprise that what she now wanted would be very costly. Snakebite had slipped back into the lunch line, returning with a hoarsely whispered cryptic message. "The laundry room. Right after dinner."

Camilla ate as if it were her last meal. It just might be, she thought as she studied the solemn faces around the table. Something was up. She could feel it on the electrified air. Even the guards seemed to sense it. Out of the corner of her eye, she saw them moving restlessly around the perimeter.

The walk down to the laundry room seemed interminable. But her resolve kept her moving. Whatever Snakebite had planned, it would be worth it if she could get the retribution she so desperately needed.

The laundry was busy with worker bees. Most of them didn't look up. Only two guards kept watch. Camilla felt the hair stand up on the back of her neck as first one of the guards stepped out and then the other.

She had one of those panicky moments, pure stomach-dropping, adrenaline-surging, breath-stopping moments before two of the women who'd been folding sheets turned and came toward her.

The first blow knocked the air out of her and smashed her teeth into her lips. The second blow cracked a rib. She tasted blood and began to fight back with everything she had.

Had she been set up from the beginning? Or was this part of the plan?

Right now it didn't matter. She was fighting for her life.

THE SOUND OF a cell phone ringing took both Tag and Hud by surprise. As Tag dug his cell phone out of his pocket and started to answer it, the marshal laid a hand on his arm.

"They could be calling to trade Lily for the thumb drive," Hud said. "Agree to meet them."

The phone rang again. "Hello?"

"It's Ace." Even over the roar of the bar crowd in the background outside his office, Tag could hear fear in Lily's brother's voice. "I just got a call demanding the thumb drive or they are going to kill Lily."

"What did you tell them?"

"To call you."

"Good." He disconnected and looked at the marshal, knowing he'd been listening in. "I'm going to give them the thumb drive."

"You have it on you? Let's take it to the office and make a copy," Hud said as he got out and motioned for Tag to get in the front seat of the patrol SUV. "I need to try to reach your father and let him know what's happening. For all we know, Harlan has already rescued Lily."

Tag wasn't going to hold his breath on that one. He still couldn't get his head around his father and uncle being agents, even retired ones. His mother had to have known. Was that another reason she'd left Harlan and Montana—or the real one?

As he climbed into the front of the patrol SUV and Hud started the engine, he touched the thumb drive in his pocket and prayed. Whoever had Lily had to believe that no one had been able to break the code. Otherwise, the thumb drive was useless to them and they would have no reason to keep Lily alive.

LILY DIDN'T FEEL so shaky after she ate. She still had a horrible taste in her mouth from whatever had been on the cloth the man had forced over her mouth. And, of course, there was the fear.

She did her best to hold it down, tempering it with the knowledge that someone would be looking for her. Not Gerald. By now he would have flown back home. She realized she probably would never see him again.

Her lack of regret made her feel a little sad. She'd almost married the man, would have if he had shown up that day. Gerald didn't know it but he'd saved them both from a horrible mistake, she thought as she got up from the mattress. Her eyes had adjusted to the dim light enough that she wasn't afraid to move around. She started on the wall next to the mattress on the floor and, moving like a blind woman, felt her way around the room.

She wasn't sure exactly what she hoped to find. Another door other than the one she'd heard the man lock behind him? A window? Anything that would give her a chance of escaping?

The room was larger than she'd thought, cleared of

any furniture. The knotty-pine walls made her think it was someone's cabin that was seldom used and that she was in the old, musty basement.

Lily tried to picture where it might be, but she had no idea how long the men had driven to get her here. Nor did she know what time of day it was. Or even what day since she didn't know how long she'd been out. She still felt groggy as she slid her fingers along the wall and took tentative steps.

She no longer wore a watch. She depended on her cell phone for the time. Her phone was in her purse, wherever that was now.

"Ouch." Her fingers connected with a wooden frame. A door frame? No, she realized as she felt around it. A window. She felt cloth and jerked. Dark fabric tore away from a basement window, bringing with it a choking amount of dust. She'd been right. This basement hadn't been used for some time.

With the window uncovered, Lily had hoped for more light. But unfortunately the snow had covered the dirty glass. Still, it was a little brighter inside the room without the dark curtain.

One look at the size of the window and she saw that it wasn't an avenue of escape. She was slim, but not slim enough to get out the window even if snow hadn't been banked up against it.

Taking advantage of the dim light, she quickly moved around the rest of the room, discovering another window and tearing off the cloth that had been tacked up over it. Less snow was banked against this one so it let in a little more light.

She could see the entire room. Definitely a basement. Musty and old and unused. Whose? Did the men who'd brought her here even know? It could be some cabin that no one used anymore.

When she reached the door, she tried the knob but of course found it locked. As she moved back to the bed, she felt her fear increase. She couldn't see how she could possibly escape this room unless she could outsmart her captors.

She had just sat down on the mattress to consider how she might do that when she remembered the sound of the man unlocking the door. No dead bolt. He'd used a key and it had made an odd sound. She stared at the door. It was very old, the wood a dark patina, so old it had a skeleton key.

Quickly she moved to the door and bent down to peer into the keyhole. There were two things about skeleton keys that gave her hope. One was that they fit in a rather loose-locking mechanism. Two was that they were often left in the other side of the door.

She could see the end of the key and the light around where it didn't quite fill the keyhole. At the sound of heavy footfalls, she scrambled toward the bed, stumbling over something. Her purse?

Grabbing it, she quickly searched for her cell phone. Gone, of course.

Hearing someone approaching, she sat down on the mattress and tucked the purse behind her to wait, her mind alive with an idea.

AT THE MARSHAL'S office, Hud copied the thumb drive onto his computer, then made a copy for Tag. "I'm going to have to keep the original."

Tag insisted on checking to make sure it had copied the information before he agreed. Then Hud told him to wait just outside his door while he made a couple of calls.

He'd started to protest, but the marshal cut him off. "Don't make me lock you up, okay? I'm going to try to reach your father. If you get the call, don't answer it until you let me know."

Tag nodded. He had little choice since all he could do was wait for Lily's abductors to call. Looking for her would be like looking for a needle in a haystack. There were too many places they could have taken her.

All he could think about was that two women had been killed and the killers had Lily. He could feel the clock ticking. He clutched the thumb drive in his pocket and prayed that they wouldn't find out that Lily had decoded what was on it.

He was too nervous to sit still. Getting up, he walked down the short hall until he was just outside the marshal's office. He could see Hud on the phone, his back to him. The door was partially open and as he moved toward it, he heard what Hud was saying.

Tag stopped, frozen in place as he listened.

"Ray Emery, huh? Okay, give me the directions to his ex's house." He repeated them as he wrote them down.

Tag recalled the name Ray Emery had been on the murder list as one of the former inmates. Ray apparently had an ex-wife who lived just outside Big Sky.

Whoever was on the other end of the line must have given him an order because Hud said, "I don't like locking him up, even for his own good…I know. I can't do anything until he gets the call…Don't worry, I won't let him play hero, but I'm doing it my way now…Yeah? So arrest me. This is your mess, Harlan. Your name is on that list next, and mine's after that…Yeah, I'll do that."

Tag had heard enough. His father wanted Hud to lock him up in jail. Once the call came in…

When the marshal hung up, he quickly placed another call. This one to the Bozeman office requesting assistance. He would need two deputies to escort someone to the airport and make sure he made the flight.

Tag didn't have to guess who that would be. He eased down the hall and let himself out the back door. Fortunately someone from the funeral had seen that Harlan's old pickup was returned to Big Sky.

Tag had seen it parked out in back of the marshal's office when they'd driven up. The keys weren't in the ignition or even on the floorboard. But Tag knew where his father kept a spare one. Their mother had learned the trick from Harlan, apparently while the two were married.

He opened the small lid over the gas cap and felt around, smiling as his fingers closed around the key.

Within minutes, he was driving out of Big Sky, headed for Ray Emery's ex-wife's house down the canyon.

WILMA EMERY LIVED in an old cabin off the road in an isolated area on the river. The cabin was pre–Big Sky and the resort, when a lot of people had summer places that were rustic, basic and far from pretentious. This was one of them.

The cabin backed up to the river and was hidden from the road by trees. Tag parked in a wide plowed spot nearby, got out and walked over to look at the river. The land was much higher here than the water.

There was a narrow trail that wound down to the water, one no doubt used by fishermen in the summer.

Now it was snow-packed, but there were tracks where some hard-core fisherman had gone down recently and fished in an open area before the surface had frozen over again.

Tag took the trail, half sliding in the snow because the embankment was a steep wall of rock and snow. He landed feetfirst on a large snowcapped rock at the river's edge.

He felt thankful he hadn't ended up breaking through the ice at the edge. As he glanced to the south where the water curved away, he couldn't see Wilma's cabin. But he knew about where it should be. He made his way across the icy round granite boulders, headed in that direction.

As he reached a point where he guessed the cabin should be just up the steep embankment, he spotted another narrow winding path upward.

The path was full of snow, almost indistinguishable. He kept thinking of Lily, his heart quickening, his stomach dropping. He had to find her. Those words were like a mantra in his ears as he scaled the embankment, slowing toward the top. He'd gotten her into this. He had to get her out.

The cabin was completely surrounded by trees. He stopped behind one large pine, its boughs low and thick, concealing him from view of the windows he'd glimpsed on this side of the cabin.

He listened, not sure what he hoped to hear. Lily screaming? That thought sent ice down his spine. As he moved toward the cabin, he thought of Lily naked in his arms last night. The woman had gotten under his skin as no woman ever had before. He would find her. He just prayed it would be soon enough.

Why hadn't the kidnappers called?

HUD HAD BEEN wondering if he was doing the right thing about Tag Cardwell as he came out from making the calls. "I still couldn't reach your father..." The rest of the lie died on his lips.

Tag was gone.

Hud swore as he hurried out to the dispatcher. "What happened to my prisoner?"

Annie looked up in surprise. "Your prisoner? It wasn't like he was handcuffed or booked..."

Hud didn't wait for the rest. He knew Annie was right. He'd screwed up. Tag had to have known he was going to be either detained in jail or shipped out of state on some other type of security warrant.

He couldn't worry about Tag now. He had to find Lily McCabe before he got the call that another woman had been murdered. He felt a sudden surge of that old feeling of wanting to put the bad guys away, that whole incredibly dangerous and yet amazing need to fight for good over evil, with the belief that he was born to do this.

He'd thought he'd lost it. He'd thought he'd needed to turn in his star because he wasn't up to doing this anymore. It made him furious with himself that he'd had these months of self-doubt. He would go down fighting because in his heart this was who he was. He couldn't escape this any more than he could escape whatever had led him down this path to begin with.

Ray Emery's ex lived down the canyon in a cabin on the river. He was betting she knew where her ex-con husband was. Emery's name was on the list.

Hud's cell phone vibrated. He checked the number. Harlan. Hud hesitated only a moment before he answered the call. "I don't know where your son is," he said into the phone. "He's like his old man. Stubborn and determined."

Harlan swore.

"I'm on my way to see Ray Emery's ex now," Hud said. "If you see Tag again, lock him up."

"Don't worry, I will." He hung up and just hoped Tag Cardwell didn't get himself killed. Assaulting an officer would hold Tag for maybe a few hours, but as determined as Harlan's son was to find Lily, Hud knew he'd be out as soon as he could call a lawyer.

But hopefully all of this would be over by then.

LILY PICKED UP HER PURSE.

Moments ago the man in the mask had come down and taken her tray and brought her another bottle of water. Again, neither of them had spoken. She'd waited until he was gone before she moved to the window with the most light.

She'd just assumed the men who took her would have taken her purse. Digging through it, she saw that other than her cell phone, nothing seemed to be missing—not even the papers Gerald had decoded the names onto.

Her heart began to pound hard. Surely they would have searched her purse for the computer flash drive. They must have ignored the papers with the names. She noticed in the dim light that Gerald had scratched out some of the letters she'd had down, replacing them with others.

She frowned. That was odd. He'd changed all the names but a couple of them. If she'd had the code wrong, wouldn't those have had to be changed, as well?

TAG HAD JUST reached the corner of the cabin when he picked up the sound of an approaching vehicle. Through the trees he watched the marshal's car pull up out front. He waited until he heard Hud pound at the front door before he edged to the back of the cabin.

Through the dust-coated window he could make out what used to be an old screened-in porch that had been entirely closed in.

He moved to the door and tried it. The knob turned, and the door groaned as he pulled it just open enough to slip in.

The back porch smelled musty. He moved to the rear door, settled his hand on the knob and prayed it, too, would be unlocked. That was what was amazing about most rural places in Montana. People didn't feel the need to lock their doors.

The door opened and he felt his heart soar. The hinges creaked softly as he slipped through. He could hear voices. Hud's deep voice. A woman's higher shrill one.

Tag found himself standing in a short hallway. He moved quickly to the first closed door, opened it. Junk room. Second door, bedroom. Third door, bathroom.

By then he could see the small cluttered living room, off it, a kitchen table and the strong smell of burned coffee.

The marshal and the woman were arguing, the woman's voice rising and falling. He could make out most of what was being said.

"I told you. I don't know where Ray is and I don't care. He won't be coming back here. He knows better than to try."

"I know you're still in contact with him," Hud argued. "You visited him just two weeks ago."

"To make sure he knew he wasn't coming back here," she snapped, voice rising again. "I'm not the criminal here. You don't have the right to come here and threaten me."

"I'm not threatening you, Wilma. Two women have been murdered. Another is missing. If Ray is involved—"

"It's his business, none of mine. That's all I have to say to you."

Tag heard the creak of the old door as she started to close it.

"If you hear from him—" The door closed.

Tag tiptoed quickly back down the hallway. He realized he wouldn't be able to reach the back door, so he slipped into the junk room.

He could hear the woman muttering under her breath and the moan of the wooden floor under her feet. It sounded as if she'd gone into the living room. To watch from the window to make sure Hud was leaving?

Silence, and then the creak and moan of the floor. She was dialing someone on her cell phone. He could hear that distinctive *beep, beep, beep* with each number she touched, then the sound of ringing.

He realized she must be standing just outside his door in the hallway by her bedroom.

"The marshal was just here," she said by way of introduction when the other end answered. Silence, then, "You *know* what I told him. That I didn't know where you were. He knew I'd come to see you just before you got out." Another beat. "No, he left. I need my money. No, I don't want to come up there. You know how I hate that road."

More silence. He heard her grunt a couple of times, then argue that she was coming to get what was hers.

"Fine. I'll wait until dark, and then I'll drive up... Why do you say that?...Stop being so paranoid. So your name is on some list. What does that prove?...Stop yelling at me. You're the one who got us into this." She sighed and he heard the creak and groan of her footfalls as she moved away.

He held his breath, thinking what the marshal had said to him on their way back into town earlier. "You're not trained for this. You have no idea what you're getting yourself into, just how dangerous it is."

Tag had mentally argued that he did know. But at this moment, he had to admit, he was just starting to realize how out of his league he really was.

Chapter Thirteen

Hud had planned to wait around and see if Wilma Emery made a move. He figured if she knew where her husband was, she might go to him. Or at least contact him.

But as he drove away down the road and pulled over, he got a call from his father-in-law.

"I've got some news," Angus said. "Can you meet me at your house?"

Hud figured if Angus talked to Harlan, he knew about the list, knew that his son-in-law's name was on it. "I'll be right there."

He drove home, ready to pack up his family and send them anywhere that might be safe. He wasn't running because he knew there was no place he would ever feel safe. He felt more alive than he had in months.

When he walked into his house, he saw that Angus hadn't said anything to his daughter about what was going on. No doubt he was waiting for Hud to tell her about the murder list and about his name being on it.

"Dad is back from his business trip," Dana said when he came through the door.

"I can see that. Honey, I need to talk to your dad...."

"I should check on the kids," Dana said, getting to her feet.

Hud was surprised she would leave them alone so quickly. It wasn't like her. He saw her send a curious glance toward them as she climbed the stairs, but she said nothing more. Nor did he and Angus until they heard her close the upstairs bedroom door.

He turned on his father-in-law. "If this is about the list—"

Angus was on his feet, finger to his lips, head cocked toward the kitchen.

Hud followed him. "Lily McCabe is missing. Tag has taken off looking for her only God knows where," he whispered once they were in the kitchen. "I'm sure Harlan told you about the list." He pulled the paper from his pocket and shoved it at his father-in-law. "Lily Mc-Cabe was decoding it."

He couldn't help being angry because he'd come into this so late. Until Mia Duncan had died, he thought both Angus and Harlan were out of this business. He'd had no idea that they were still involved in these kinds of things. Like Dana, he didn't pay much attention when either came or went. Until now.

"You should have trusted me," he said as he watched Angus take in the names on the paper. He didn't seem surprised—not even that his son-in-law's name was there.

Paul Brown was dead. Hud hadn't wanted to believe these lists even existed. But now he was staring the truth in the face. Worse, he didn't know who would be coming after him.

After a moment, Angus turned on the water, just letting it run into the sink, before he answered. "Where did you get this list?"

Hud told him what Tag had told him.

"Do you have the thumb drive?"

"Yes, but Tag has a copy. He plans to trade it for Lily."

Angus nodded. "This list," he said, wadding up the paper in his hand and tossing it into the garbage, "isn't the right one."

"What?"

"Lily McCabe must have decoded it wrong or Mia passed the wrong one."

Hud raked a hand through his hair. "Then my name isn't on the list?" He saw the answer in his father-in-law's expression and swore under his breath.

"Harlan's in Billings at the women's prison."

Hud felt his stomach roil. "You're telling me Camilla is the one who put the hit out on me?" He knew that shouldn't have come as a surprise, not after what had happened the day Camilla was sentenced.

As she was being taken from the room, she was led past him. She stopped just inches from him.

"I will get you if it's the last thing I do," she whispered through one of her innocent smiles. "You *and* your family." Then she'd laughed as they'd dragged her away. He'd been hearing that laugh in his sleep for months.

Angus met his gaze. "It's more complicated than that."

There was both compassion and fear in the older man's gaze. Hud didn't even need to hear the rest. He knew. He'd known deep in his soul that this wasn't over. That it wouldn't be over until that crazy woman was dead.

"Camilla Northland has been taken to the hospital," Angus said. "She got into an altercation with two other inmates in the laundry room. Harlan hasn't been able

to talk to her yet. But with this hit out on you, we need
to get Dana and the kids out of here."

TUGGING OFF HIS Stetson, Hud ran a hand through his
hair. The sun had set, and deep shadows had filled in
under the pines.

"How do you suggest we get your wife and children
away from here two days before Christmas?" Angus
asked.

He knew his wife. "We have to tell her the truth. She
has a right to know. She's strong. She'll—"

"She won't leave you, you should know that."

"Yes, he should know that," Dana said from the
kitchen doorway.

DARKNESS CAME ON quickly in the canyon. From a silky
gray as the sun passed behind Lone Mountain, the canyon took on a chill even in the summer.

In the winter once the sun was gone, the canyon
became an icebox. Even if the snow on the roads had
thawed during a warm December day, the melt now
froze solid, the roads suddenly becoming ice-skating
rinks.

Tag didn't see the dark coming, but he felt it. Wilma
Emery had been moving restlessly around the cabin.
He thought he heard her packing, the closet door in the
bedroom across the hall opening, the *ting* of metal hang-
ers as clothes were pulled off them, then the sound of
dresser drawers being opened and closed.

She dragged something heavy from the bedroom
and down the hall toward the front door. He knew he
would have to move fast once she left. Not the river
route he'd taken to get here. He would have to reach

his father's pickup quickly if he hoped to tail her. He couldn't lose her.

He heard the front door open, followed by a series of grunts and groans and bumps and scrapes; then the door slammed shut.

Tag counted to five and opened the storeroom door. No sound came from the front of the cabin. Hurriedly he moved to the living room and peeked out of a crack in the curtains.

A solid-looking woman was shoving a huge duffel bag into the back of an older dark-colored large Suburban.

He hurried out through the back, the way he'd come in, and worked his way along the side of the cabin in time to see her go back into the cabin. He knew he was taking a chance, but he rushed down the road toward where he'd left his father's truck.

Behind him he heard the sound of an engine kick over. The dual golden beams of headlights shot across the frozen expanse to his left. He rushed into the pines and hurriedly climbed behind the wheel of the old pickup. As he slid down in the seat, the lights of the Suburban washed through the cab.

He held his breath, listening, half expecting the Suburban to slow, and then stop. There was no doubt in his mind that Wilma Emery was armed and dangerous. Or that he was in over his head.

But she didn't slow, didn't stop and a moment later the cab of the pickup went dark again. He sat up, heart pounding. As the Suburban headed out the narrow snowy unpaved road, he noticed that the right taillight had burned out.

Tag doubted that the woman would check her rearview mirror, but he couldn't take the chance. He waited until Wilma was almost to the highway.

He'd purposely left the key in the ignition, afraid he might lose it on his hike along the river to the cabin.

Now he pressed down on the clutch and brake and turned the key as he watched the Suburban turn onto the highway. The engine groaned but didn't turn over.

"Don't do this," he said to the truck. "Not now." He tried again. The engine groaned. "No!" He could see Wilma getting away. She was headed to meet her husband—and Ray Emery had Lily. He was sure of it.

He prayed that the pickup would start and tried it again. The engine groaned, but sparked and turned over. It was feeble. The cold engine vibrated the whole pickup as it rumbled.

Tag feared it would die and not start again, but when he put it in gear and let his foot off the clutch, it lurched forward out of the pines. He didn't turn on his headlights, following the darker shadows of the ruts through the snow, until he reached the highway.

He'd seen Wilma turn left onto the highway—away from Big Sky. Tag did the same. He couldn't go too fast. The highway was shiny in his headlights when he turned them on and he could feel the tires slipping on the glaze of ice on the pavement.

The highway was a crooked snake that wriggled through the Gallatin Canyon. This far south of Big Sky, there was little traffic. Skiers would have made their way home by now.

By the second bend in the road and no sign of Wilma Emery, he was starting to panic. Had she turned off? He had been watching, but there were few side roads along here.

Another curve and he saw the one red taillight shining in the distance. His pulse began to drop back to normal. *I'm coming, Lily. Hang on.*

LILY PRAYED FOR darkness, hoping that whoever was upstairs would need sleep. She didn't dare try anything as long as they were moving around up there.

Earlier she'd heard a male voice and figured he must be talking on the phone, but she couldn't make out what he was saying. Her stomach churned at the thought of them talking about her. Talking about what to do with her.

She felt confused. She'd thought they wanted the thumb drive. It was the only thing that made sense. But if that were the case, why hadn't they taken the papers from her purse with the names on them?

And if they didn't want the thumb drive, then why were they still keeping her alive? It didn't make any sense.

She moved to the door again and peered through at the tiny spots of light around the key. She was so tempted to try to get out that if it hadn't been for the sound of footfalls upstairs, she would have tried to get the key.

Hurrying back to the mattress, she curled against the cold pine wall and stared at the door, fearing one or both of them would come down at any moment and kill her.

At the sound of a door slamming upstairs, she froze. Had he left? She waited, praying that he'd left her here alone, because from what she could tell, there was only one man upstairs. She'd seen only one man since she'd been grabbed in the parking lot of the motel.

She heard a door open and close again, then the creak of the floorboards over her head, and knew she wasn't alone. She hugged herself and waited for the darkness outside the window to settle in and hopefully lull her abductor to sleep.

"TELL ME," DANA said as she stepped into the kitchen.

Hud saw her grab the edge of the kitchen table as if she knew she was going to need to hang on to something. He looked at his father-in-law, then at his wife. Dana was strong. She'd weathered many storms on this ranch. She'd single-handedly fought her siblings for the land that was her legacy.

"Someone has put a hit out on me," he said simply.

She nodded, glanced toward the kitchen window. A nervous laugh escaped her lips. She quickly quelled it. "Dee. I mean Camilla." Camilla had come to them pretending to be Dee Ann Justice, a long-lost cousin. "She's the one who put the hit on you, isn't she?"

When Hud didn't answer, she glanced at her father.

"We think it's a possibility," Angus said. His cell phone rang. "I have to take this." He stepped out of the room.

"Do you know who?"

"Apparently some inmates have gotten together and started a co-op type of murder list," Hud said, ignoring the disapproving look Angus gave him from just outside the kitchen. "It will probably be an ex-inmate coming for me. That's why you need to take the kids and leave. Go to my father's. I can call Brick—"

Dana shook her head. "We're safer here, especially if Camilla is involved. She knows everything about us, remember? The first place she would look for us would be Brick's—if she didn't have someone lying in wait for us along the way to West Yellowstone."

Angus stepped back into the room. "I'm sorry, but I have to go."

Hud nodded. Dana studied her father, and then quickly moved to plant a kiss on his cheek.

"Be careful," she whispered.

"Will you two be—"

"We'll manage," Hud snapped, then softened his tone with his father-in-law as he said, "Go. We'll be fine."

"We will be fine," Dana said, and stepped into her husband's arms. Hud held her tight, more afraid than he wanted to admit that they wouldn't be fine. Far from it.

TAG'S PULSE POUNDED in his ears as he stayed back just enough that he would catch sight of the one red taillight every few turns.

At the mouth of the canyon, Wilma slowed, crossed the bridge and turned onto the old river road.

Tag pulled off just before the bridge in a wide spot and waited. He could see her taillight for some distance now. He waited until he couldn't stand it anymore, then crossed the bridge and turned down the narrow old road.

Out of the canyon now, he could see stars in the clear night sky. They glittered from the midnight-blue canopy overhead. As he drove, the moon came up from behind the mountains to the east, a bright white orb that lit the fallen snow.

Ahead, Wilma's taillight blinked as she braked and turned down a road that led toward the river. He lost sight of her in the thick cottonwoods, but he knew she couldn't go far before she ran into the river.

He found a place up the road to pull over, then started to climb out of the pickup. Hud's words came back to him again. He had no idea what he was going to find down that road.

On a hunch, he reached under the pickup's seat. He found an ax handle. All kinds of other junk. No old pistol. He was disappointed in his father. Nor was there a shotgun or even a .22 rifle hanging from the rack behind the seat.

He tried the glove box and was about to give up and see if he could find at least a tire iron, when he noticed something interesting about the passenger-side floorboard.

He lifted a flap in the rubber mat and saw the handle. When he lifted it, he found more than he'd hoped for.

Until that moment, he hadn't really believed his father was an agent of any kind.

But as he pulled out a Glock handgun, then a sawed-off shotgun—both loaded—he became a believer. Sticking the Glock into the back waistband of his jeans, he hoisted the shotgun, grabbed a pocketful of shells and headed down the road.

Chapter Fourteen

There were two things Tag's father had taught his older
sons before they left Montana—to swim and to shoot
a gun.

"I'm not having one of my boys drowning in the river
because he can't swim," Harlan had told their mother.
"And they're going to learn to shoot."

"They're too young," she'd cried as he loaded them
into the pickup.

They'd learned to swim in a small deep eddy down in
the Gallatin on a warm summer day. Not that the water
had been warm. Rivers and lakes in most of Montana
never warmed up that much.

But each of them had learned. His father's method
hadn't been exactly mother approved. He'd tossed them
in one at a time. Sink or swim. They'd learned to swim,
kicking and screaming.

With shooting that hadn't been the case. They were
boys, after all. Harlan had been strict about safety as
well as learning how to load, clean and shoot a gun.

Now as Tag approached the 1940s-looking cabin, he
snapped off the safety on the shotgun.

The snow crunched under his feet as he walked. He
thought about calling the marshal. Not until he knew
for certain that Lily was down here. He still wasn't

sure he could trust Hud. The man had been ready to put him on a plane.

Without a cloud in the night sky, the temperature had dropped. His breath came out frosty and white. The moon lit the land, making the snow look like white marble. In the cottonwoods, deep shadows filled the road's ruts. It was hard to see where he was walking. A couple of times he slipped in the icy tracks and almost fell but managed to catch himself.

Tag thought of his brothers. They wouldn't believe it if they saw him, armed and tromping through a dark, snowy night to save a woman. He'd had relationships. He'd just never met a woman who he would have been tromping through a dark and snowy night to save.

Worse, he and Lily didn't even have a relationship. Hell, for all he knew she was planning to go back to her former fiancé. Jealousy dug under his skin at the thought.

Either way, he had to find her.

Ahead, he spotted Wilma's SUV parked in front of the cabin, only this one had a basement. One lone light burned in a window close to the ground at the other end of the building. Inside the house proper, lights blazed.

Tag glanced around. There was no other vehicle. That bothered him. Had someone left but was planning to be back at any time? That seemed more likely than that whoever Wilma had talked to was staying here without transportation.

The thought made him nervous. It was that ticking clock he'd been hearing in his ear since he'd realized Lily was missing. But now it seemed to be ticking even faster.

Move.

He did, through the deep snow, toward the corner

of the house that was the darkest. He could smell the river bottom, the scent of decayed leaves that haunted every riverbed.

As he drew nearer to the house, he could hear raised voices, a woman's and a man's. Edging along the side of the house, he got as close to the front window as he could without being seen.

He took a quick peek. Wilma and the man he'd seen help Mia into a pickup that night behind the bar. The two were standing at the edge of the living room arguing. The man had a gun in his hand. He appeared to be threatening Wilma with it.

Tag's cell phone vibrated in his pocket, making him jump.

CAMILLA KNEW IT was just a matter of time before Marshal Hud Savage learned that she had escaped from the hospital.

She would have liked to check into a motel for a few days, get her strength back, heal. But she couldn't chance it. As bad a shape as she was in from her beating, checking into a motel the way she looked would be dangerous. Not only that, but it would give Hud time to get ready for her.

True to her word, Snakebite had seen that everything she needed had been waiting for her on the outside. She had a vehicle, weapons and what tools she might need. She smiled even though it hurt her mouth to do so.

By now the marshal would have heard that she had been taken to the hospital. He was too smart not to know she might be using it to escape. That Hud would be expecting the worst made it all the more delicious. She had to assume the marshal's office would be guarded.

So would the ranch house. Fortunately, Hud was a lawman through and through. His one Achilles' heel was that he couldn't resist anyone in trouble.

She'd gotten word that he would soon be headed for a cabin down the canyon where a woman named Lily McCabe was being held captive. Camilla was in awe of the working prison network. Hud being called away from the house would buy her valuable time to take care of a few things in his absence.

That and the fact that she knew the ranch layout—even in the dead of night—would make her plan work. She didn't need to worry about getting away. The worst they could do to her was lock her up again. She was already looking at life in prison. There was no way Hud would ever have let her get paroled, and now that she'd escaped, even more years would be added on to her sentence.

If only Hud had wanted her, she thought. They could have been happy together. He would have gotten over the loss of Dana and the kids. At least that was what she'd told herself last spring. She'd wanted him. Deserved a man like him. She'd thought her life would have been so different if a good man had come into it sooner.

But he hadn't wanted her. He'd wanted Dana. She made a face at the memory of sweet Dana and her children. They were always baking cookies and making a racket. And Hud… A hard knot formed high in her chest at the memory of how he had rejected her. The one man she would have done anything for, and he'd rejected her.

Camilla pushed those thoughts away as she drove toward the Gallatin Canyon. She had a mission. Hud would soon know she was coming. She smiled. He just wouldn't be expecting what she had planned for him.

TAG'S PHONE VIBRATED again. He felt his heart quicken as he realized that the man and woman inside the house weren't on a phone.

He edged away from the window and into the nearby pines, answering the phone on its third ring.

"Hello." He waited. He could hear someone breathing on the other end of line. "What?" he demanded.

"Don't be so impatient."

He didn't recognize the voice as he moved so he had a view of the living room—and the two people standing nearby in the kitchen doorway. They were both facing each other, still having a serious talk.

Tag had to assume the person on the phone wasn't inside this building.

Who the devil was this on the phone, then?

"What do you want?" he asked, stepping back into the snowy pines out of sight.

"You know what I want."

"Do I?"

A low chuckle.

"What about what I want?" Tag asked, half afraid of saying Lily's name. What if there were more people looking for the thumb drive than he knew?

"Your girlfriend?"

He breathed a sigh of relief even though Lily was far from his girlfriend. Then he had a thought. "What makes you think she's my girlfriend?"

Another chuckle. "I was giving you the benefit of the doubt after what I saw through her bedroom window last night."

His heart dropped at the realization that the man who'd run him off the road had followed him to Lily's. He hadn't seen anyone, but he'd left tracks in the falling snow. He'd led the man right to Lily.

"I want to know that she's all right," Tag said. "Let me talk to her."

"That isn't an option right now even though I can assure you, she is fine."

"Not good enough." He'd seen enough movies to know he needed to have proof that she was still alive. What he really wanted to know was if the man was in the house—and if not, where was he?

"Give me a little time," the man said on the other end of the line. "Ten minutes. Then I'll call you back. You'd better have what I want." The man disconnected.

Tag could still hear the two in the house arguing. He quickly backtracked down the side of the house and around to the back. He heard nothing at any of the windows, but when he reached the basement one with the lone light, he bent down, dug away some of the snow and peered in.

What he saw made his heart beat faster. A tray with a consumed TV dinner on it, an empty bottle of water and a used napkin.

Lily was here. He knew it.

He moved to one of the dark basement windows. As he cleared away the snow, he saw that the glass opening was small. Too small for a person to climb out.

He bent down and tried to peer in. The glass was filthy. He wiped at it with a handful of snow and heard a sound on the other side. Stepping back out of sight, he watched the window out of the corner of his eye. A hand touched the glass. A small, female hand.

Tag quickly bent down again. The basement room was too dark for him to see more than a shadowy figure at first. Then she put her face nearer to the glass and he saw her. His heart almost burst from his chest.

DANA HAD GONE upstairs to check on the kids when Hud's cell phone rang. He took the call even though he didn't recognize the number.

"I know where Lily McCabe is," the woman's voice on the other end of the line said.

"Who is this?" He recognized the voice. Wilma Emery. But he didn't call her on it, fearing she might hang up.

"Never mind that. They're holding her at a cabin." The woman gave him hurried directions. "You better make it fast or they will kill her like they—" There was what sounded like a struggle, and then the line went dead.

Hud swore as he disconnected and looked up as his wife came down the stairs.

"What is it?" she asked.

"Wilma Emery just called. She sounded scared. She told me where they're holding Lily McCabe. I don't like the way the call ended."

Dana's eyes widened in alarm as her hand went to her mouth. "What if this is only a ruse to get you to…" Tears filled her eyes.

"I can't leave you and the kids."

She made quick swipe at her tears and seemed to pull herself together, the way she always did when the going got tough. "You have to go. The kids and I will be fine."

His cell phone rang again. He swore when he saw it was Tag Cardwell calling. "Where are you?" he demanded as he stepped out of the kitchen and earshot of his wife.

"I've found Lily."

Hud listened as Tag gave him the same directions to the cabin on the river that Wilma had given him.

"I'll be right there. Just wait. Don't do anything, do you hear me?"

Tag didn't answer and Hud realized he'd hung up. With a curse, he looked to his wife.

"Go."

He knew he had no choice. He was still the marshal. "Please, Dana, I need you to leave with the kids. Get packed while I'm gone."

"Camilla's in the hospital. They'd let us know if she wasn't." She stepped to him, drawing him into a tight hug. "You just worry about coming back to us safe and sound."

"Always."

CAMILLA FINISHED TAPING her ribs in the filling station bathroom. The antiseptic smell of the recently cleaned restroom made her hold her breath. Not that breathing was all that easy with her cracked ribs.

How long before the hospital realized she was gone? She smiled since her ruse would have bought her time.

As she let her gaze lift to the metal mirror over the sink, she was startled because she didn't recognize herself. Her face was swollen and bruised in shades of grays and yellows. Her right eye was black and almost swollen shut.

There was still dried blood on the cut on her upper lip. She was missing a front tooth.

Camilla let out a small laugh, which she quickly killed because it hurt her chest.

"How do you think you're going to do anything as messed up as you are?" she asked the woman in the mirror.

The clock was ticking since she knew every cop in

the state would be looking for her soon. She'd split right away from the other inmate she'd escaped with.

There wasn't safety in numbers—not with them looking as bad as they did. She'd held her own in the fight and done as much damage as she could. She also knew she would attract less attention on her own.

Her face would heal. So would her cracked ribs. But she couldn't take the time. She had everything she needed: a vehicle, money, weapons. The problem was everyone would know where she was heading.

"You could get out of the country," she told her reflection. "You don't have to do this."

Her eyes narrowed at the thought. "You could go to some warm tropical place and sip tropical drinks with the locals." She smiled at the thought, but knew that wasn't her M.O.

She couldn't live with herself if she didn't finish this. Hud would be expecting her to come for him—especially after he heard about the prison break.

He would whisk Dana and the kids off somewhere, thinking they would be safe. Hud wouldn't run, she thought with a lopsided smile. He would think he could best her at whatever she had planned for him.

She loved nothing better than a challenge. Even beat up and in pain, she felt up to it. Hud would be off saving some other damsel in distress. It would give her plenty of time to take care of things at the ranch before he returned.

She could hardly contain her excitement at seeing Hud Savage again. *Soon, Hud.*

TAG KNELT DOWN by the window. Lily was trying to tell him something, but he couldn't hear her. He motioned for her to move back. He could still hear Wilma and the man he suspected was her ex-husband, Ray Emery, arguing even more loudly from another part of the cabin.

He hoped they were far enough away and the basement deep enough that they wouldn't hear what he was about to do. Wrapping the butt of the shotgun around the tail end of his coat, he leaned down and smashed the glass. The sound felt like a gunshot, it was so loud to him.

He listened, afraid the others had heard it. But with staggering relief, he heard the two inside the house still arguing.

"Are you all right?" he asked the moment Lily appeared at the small broken window. He could see her, but he ached to take her in his arms. It was the only way he could convince himself that she truly was all right.

She nodded, looking scared but definitely relieved to see him.

"How many people are in the house?"

She shook her head. "Someone left earlier. I've only seen one man, but I heard someone come a little while ago. It sounds like a woman."

So there was just the redheaded man and Wilma.

"I think the one just got out of prison."

He could feel the cold seeping in through the knees of his jeans as he knelt on the ground. Time was passing. The man on the phone said he would call back in ten minutes—and let him talk to Lily. He had to move quickly.

"I know how you feel about guns, but I'm afraid you're going to need this," he said as he pulled the Glock from behind him and handed it to her through the window. "It's ready to go. All you have to do is pull the trigger. Aim for the largest part of the body." He saw her cringe. "You can do this."

She nodded, a determined look settling on her features.

He gave her a smile, then pulled off his glove and reached through the broken window to touch her face with his fingertips. She closed her eyes, leaning into his warm palm. Tears beaded her lashes when he pulled his hand away.

"I'll be down to get you in a few minutes. If anyone else comes through the door, shoot them."

With that, he stood. From inside the house came the loud report of a gunshot followed by a scream and another gunshot. Tag grabbed the shotgun and ran toward the front of the house.

LILY LISTENED. She heard nothing overhead following the two gunshots and the scream. Her heart was beating like a war drum. Tag had come for her. She'd known he would. He was that kind of cowboy. Wasn't that why she'd made love with him last night? She'd known the kind of man he was. Otherwise, she would never have—

Another gunshot and the pounding of footfalls. She held her breath as she looked toward the door, then down at the gun in her hand. Her heart was in her throat now. Was Tag all right? He'd come to save her, but what if—

She couldn't bear to let herself even think it.

She had to get out of here. She couldn't just stand here waiting for that door to open. Dropping the gun onto the mattress, she moved to the door, willing her trembling to stop.

When she'd heard someone at the window, she'd been just about to push the piece of paper she'd written the codes on under the door. In a perfect world, once she pushed the key through from her side, it would fall on the sheet of paper and she would pull it through. Once she had the key, she could open the door.

This wasn't like any mathematical problem she'd ever come across. This was her life. She didn't know why they had kept her alive. But she feared all of that had now changed. They would kill her and Tag if they got the chance.

She'd held her breath, waiting and praying that the next sound she heard was Tag's voice on the other side of the door.

But there had been nothing.

Lily didn't know how long she'd waited. Until she couldn't take it any longer.

Finally she pushed the sheet of paper slowly under the door, her heart in her throat. She half expected the paper to be jerked away, the door to fly open…

But nothing happened.

Now, willing her fingers not to tremble, she used the piece of plastic fork she'd kept to carefully poke gently into the keyhole.

She felt the key move. If she pushed too hard, the key would fall out—away from the door and the paper she'd pushed under the door.

Too slowly and she chanced that someone would come downstairs—someone other than Tag.

She pushed and prayed and a moment later she heard the key fall and land with a *clink*.

Her heart dropped. It sounded as if the key had missed the sheet of paper. Now it would be out of her reach.

She could barely stand even the thought as she knelt down to see where the key had gone. To her shock, she saw it lying half on, half off the paper.

Her fingers were trembling too hard for her to touch the sheet of paper and try to pull it back inside the room.

She took deep breaths. She had one chance. She stilled her trembling as she knelt farther down and at a snail's pace, she began to pull the corner of the paper with the key hanging off it toward her.

The light caught on the key. It flashed, so close now that she could almost feel it in her hand when she opened the door.

A huge foot suddenly stomped down on the key and sheet of paper. She let out a scream before she could catch herself and fell back on her butt.

As the man put the key in the lock and threw open the door, she scuttled backward, unable to get her feet under her quickly enough to stand.

The large man loomed over her, sans his mask. The light caught on the gun in his hand as he raised it, the barrel pointed at her chest.

"You're too smart for your own good," the man said.

The gunshot was deafening in the basement room. Lily didn't realize that she'd closed her eyes until she opened them to find the man still standing over her.

He had an odd expression on his face.

Lily looked down expecting to see blood, expecting to feel life leaking from her. When she saw nothing, she looked back up in time to see him falling toward her.

She rolled away at the last instant. As he fell face-first within inches of her, she saw the hole in the back of his shirt and the blood seeping out.

As a shadow filled the doorway, her gaze swung to it. The next moment she was in Tag's arms and he was holding her. "We have to get out of here," Tag whispered next to her ear, but he moved as if he couldn't bear letting her go.

She nodded against his chest, then drew back to look at the man lying on the basement floor. "Is he…?"

Tag didn't answer. He picked up the Glock from the mattress, took her hand and led her up the stairs. As they neared the top, he motioned for her to stay back.

She caught only a glimpse of a woman's body lying on the floor near the kitchen as Tag hurriedly drew her toward the outside door. "Was that—"

"Ray Emery's wife. The two of them were arguing. He killed her before I came in."

They stepped out into the cold, wintery night. The sky was ebony and adorned with tiny white jewels. A moon washed over the snow, turning it to alabaster. The freezing air stole her breath. That and the sound of a vehicle roaring toward the cabin, the lights bobbing on the rough snow-packed road.

TAG DREW LILY toward a barn on the back of the property. As they slipped into the pitch-black, he held her to him for a moment until his eyes adjusted to the light.

Now if he could just get Lily out of here. He could hear the sound of the vehicle's engine growing louder. Not the marshal. Not the way the rig was roaring down the road without flashing lights or a siren. No, it was probably whoever he'd spoken to earlier on the phone.

His eyes finally adjusted to the darkness. They fell on the large snowmobile at the door. He stepped away from Lily for a moment to feel if the key was in it. It was.

"When I start the snowmobile's engine, open the barn door the rest of the way and hop on," he told Lily as they heard two car doors slam, followed by shouts from the house moments later.

He started the snowmobile and threw it into gear, as

Lily swung the door wide. He pulled her on as he hit the gas and burst out into the freezing night.

The headlight of the snowmobile bobbed as they took off, racing through the deep snow of the field. Tag headed for a stand of pines, knowing that as long as they were in the open field, they were too perfect a target.

A bullet whizzed past.

Lily wrapped her arms around his waist as they sped across the field, the snowmobile busting through drifts and sending up a cloud of fresh snow. The air filled with ice crystals as it blew past. Moonbeams played over the surface of the fresh-fallen snow. The winter night seemed to be holding its breath.

When Tag dared look back, he saw the light of another snowmobile coming after them.

Chapter Fifteen

As Hud raced toward the cabin where Tag had said Lily McCabe was being held, the urgent call came in from Harlan.

"Camilla Northland has escaped from prison."

The words hit like a sledgehammer. He tried to breathe, to keep his heart from banging out of his chest. Ahead, he could see the turnoff into the cabin. All he managed to say was, "How long ago?"

"Four hours ago."

"Four hours! Wasn't there a guard outside her door?"

"She got the jump on him. Unfortunately there was a bus accident and the doctors and nurses were busy...."

Four hours would give Camilla plenty of time to get to where she was headed. For all he knew, Camilla was in Big Sky. Even on the ranch. There was no doubt in his mind that she would be coming after him and his family.

Hud fought to take a breath. Fear paralyzed him for a moment. Fear, and the memory of just how far that crazy psychopath of a woman would go to get what she wanted.

He touched his brakes at the turnoff and swung down the old river road. "How?"

"She'd gotten into an altercation with two other women. They were all taken to the hospital because of their injuries. Two of them escaped. Camilla was one of them."

All these months when Dana had been afraid that Camilla would find a way to come after them again, he'd told her not to worry. That Camilla was never getting out of prison. That she could never get to them again.

"She's on her way to the ranch if she isn't already there," he said, hoping Harlan could tell him otherwise.

Instead, the former agent said, "I just talked to Angus. He's headed back there now. I'm on my way, but I can send a deputy—"

"Does Dana know?"

"Angus hasn't told her yet."

"Tell him to call and tell her. I'll be there as soon as I can." He hung up. It took everything in him not to turn around and race toward the ranch. But Tag Cardwell and Lily McCabe were in the cabin ahead. He couldn't let them die even to save his own family.

Ahead he saw two snowmobiles racing toward him.

CAMILLA MOVED THROUGH the dark toward the house. Her ribs hurt. She stopped and had to shift the gun stuck in her waistband. The snow was deeper than she'd thought it would be and had worn her out quickly. Either that or she was in worse shape from the fight than she thought.

In the distance she could see the lights on at the ranch house. Had Dana heard yet that her "cousin" was on the way? Had Hud?

She'd checked before she began her hike. The marshal was still involved in the showdown by the river. Subterfuge at its best.

Camilla pushed on through the fallen snow until she reached the backside of the house. When she'd stayed here last April, she'd come and gone in the middle of the night several times. She'd learned the darkest parts of the yard and the best way to enter so as not to be seen.

Nearing the house, she slowed to catch her breath. Hud's patrol rig wasn't parked out front. She had to believe her information was correct and Hud was still involved down the canyon.

She tried the door. Locked. She smiled, realizing she would have been disappointed if Dana had left the door open for her.

She glanced at her watch. Dana was a creature of habit. She would be upstairs putting the kids to bed right now.

It took only a few moments to pick the lock and, easing the door open, slip inside.

THE WHINE OF the snowmobile behind them grew louder. Tag ventured a look back. He'd gotten Lily into this. He had to get her out. Another bullet zinged past, this one so close it took his breath away. The pines were ahead. Just a little farther and they would be in the trees.

He didn't see the dip in the snow until it was too late. The snowmobile roared down into it, but the skis caught in the deep snow and then hit the ground underneath.

Tag flung the two of them to the side as the snowmobile nose-dived. He rolled. He felt Lily slam into him as they hit the ground and were instantly covered with snow.

He came up only to be blinded by the lights of the other snowmobile. The light suddenly shut off as the sound of the snowmobile motor died and a large dark figure loomed over them.

Tag pulled her closer so his body shielded hers. He could see the shotgun lying just feet away. The snowmobile, its engine still running, its lights dim, buried in the deep snow, idled just feet away.

The moonlight caught the glint of metal as the man pulled a gun from his coat. "The two of you have caused nothing but problems," he said between gritted teeth. "All you had to do was give us the damned flash drive." He aimed the gun at Tag's chest. "Hand it over now or I'll take it off your body. Which is it going to be?"

Tag dug in his pocket and pulled out the computer thumb drive. He tossed it to the man, knowing the man would miss it. The small device fell into the deep snow, making the man swear.

Behind Tag, he felt Lily loosen her hold on him, felt her take the pistol from his pocket. She raised the gun. He could feel her trembling, the hand holding the gun shaking. The killer saw it, too. She couldn't pull the trigger.

Tag lunged for the shotgun lying next to the snowmobile in the snow. The sound of the gunshot made him flinch. He heard Lily cry out. For a moment, he thought she'd pulled the trigger. But the shot had come from farther away.

The man standing over them appeared surprised as he looked down at his chest. The gun in his hand wavered, then fell from his fingers into the deep snow. The second shot dropped the man.

Marshal Hud Savage waded toward them through the snow. Behind Tag, Lily was crying and saying, "I just couldn't pull the trigger. I just couldn't."

Tag took her in his arms, assuring her that it didn't matter, but he could tell that it did matter much more than it should have to her.

As CAMILLA CAME around the corner from the kitchen, Dana came face-to-face with the woman she'd thought was her cousin only months before.

"Dee—" She caught herself. "I'm sorry, it's Camilla, isn't it?"

"Actually I go by Spark now." She smiled but didn't raise the gun she clutched at her side.

"Cute," Dana said, still surprised how much the two of them resembled each other even though they shared no blood. It had made it so easy for Camilla to pretend to be her cousin. Dana hated how vulnerable she'd been just months ago.

"What now?" Camilla asked, still smiling.

"I guess that's up to you. I always wondered what I would do if I ever saw you again."

"Really?" Her gaze went to the shotgun in Dana's hands, the barrel aimed at her heart. "And now here we are. You know, we would have made great cousins. We're so much alike."

"We're nothing alike," Dana snapped.

Camilla's smile wasn't quite as self-assured as it had been. "Are you sure about that?" She looked past Dana. "I thought you would be putting your children to bed." She cocked her head. "I don't hear the patter of their little feet."

"They aren't here. They're with Hilde."

"Hilde, your good and loyal friend," Camilla scoffed.

"You tried to destroy that friendship, but you failed."

"I'm surprised your *good* friend would leave you, knowing what you were up to."

"I talked her into taking the children so I could get packed to leave since you'd put a hit out on my husband."

Camilla raised an eyebrow. "I don't see you packing."

"No, I've just been waiting for you. You wouldn't just want Hud. You'd come after me and my children again. I decided to get it over with."

"You were that sure I'd come here?"

Dana smiled. "I knew you couldn't let anyone else do your dirty work. You enjoy it too much."

"You might have more backbone than I thought." She glanced toward the front window. "Or you're expecting your husband to come save you."

Dana laughed softly. "You think I'm weak, certainly no match for you, since you were able to fool me so easily, isn't that right?"

Camilla didn't bother to answer, the truth in her smirk. "I bet that shotgun isn't even loaded."

Dana laughed. "Wanna bet?"

"Have you ever killed anyone?" Camilla sighed. "It's not easy. You'll have to live with what you've done."

Dana laughed again. "How would you know anything about living with what you've done? You have no conscience."

"You're wrong. I never wanted to do the things I've done. If I could do it over—"

"That won't work with me anymore," Dana interrupted. "I know you. I can see into the darkness where your soul should be."

Camilla smiled and took a step toward Dana.

"I wouldn't do that if I were you."

"You don't have what it takes. I can see it in your eyes. I'm betting I can raise my gun and fire before you have the guts to pull that trigger."

"That will be the bet of a dead woman."

Camilla stopped moving. Her fingers holding the pistol at her side twitched. "I'm beginning to see what Hud sees in you. Where is he, by the way?"

"Right behind you," Dana said.

"You expect me to fall for that? I turn around and

you jump me?" Camilla shook her head. "What we have here is a standoff. I shoot you. You shoot me."

"Except I have a shotgun which means after I shoot you, you won't be going back to prison so you can escape again and hurt someone else. Nor will I live in fear anymore. This ends here."

HUD HEARD THE shots as he raced toward the front door of his ranch house. He burst in, gun in hand, to find his wife on the floor in a pool of blood. A few feet away, Camilla Northland was struggling to get to her feet. Her left side was a mass of torn bloody fabric. But one look at her and he knew she would survive this—just as she had survived everything else in her life.

The marshal stepped to her quickly and smashed his boot heel into the hand holding the pistol. She didn't even make a sound as he kicked the gun out of the way and rushed to his wife.

"Call 911," he yelled as Tag Cardwell appeared in the open doorway. Hud had told Tag and Lily to stay in the patrol vehicle. He wasn't surprised that Tag hadn't.

"Dana," Hud cried. "Dana, can you hear me?" Leaning down, he placed his head to her chest and with a groan of relief, felt it rise and fall. She was still alive.

Tag was on the phone with the 911 operator. In the distance, Hud could hear the sound of sirens. He saw the crease along his wife's skull where the bullet had grazed her. She was losing blood fast. He quickly yanked off his jacket and shirt and pressed the shirt to her wound as a shadow fell over him.

"Look out!" Tag cried.

As Hud spun around, he instinctively picked up the shotgun lying beside his wife. Camilla loomed over him, a knife raised high. But it was the expression on her face that froze his breath in his throat. She was smiling broadly, her eyes as bright as the moonlight on the snow outside.

She drove down with the blade, aiming for his heart. He rocked back, raised the barrel and fired. As he rolled to the side at the last minute, the knife plunged past him so close he thought he'd felt the whisper of the blade, which stuck in the floor as Camilla fell on top of him. With disgust, he shoved her body aside.

Outside the ambulance's lights flashed as it swung into the yard and two EMTs jumped and ran toward the open door.

"Dana," Hud whispered next to her ear. "Don't leave me. Please don't leave me."

Chapter Sixteen

While Hud went to the hospital with his wife, a deputy marshal by the name of Jake Thorton took Tag's and Lily's statements. By now it was almost daylight.

Tag felt numb. Tomorrow was Christmas Eve. So much had happened that he couldn't imagine celebrating the holiday now. Camilla Northland was dead. His cousin Dana was in the hospital in a coma. Both Angus and Harlan were tying up the loose ends of the murder list case.

"I almost got you killed," Lily had said on the way to the marshal's office. She looked and sounded exhausted. There was a haunted look in her eyes that Tag had desperately wanted to exorcise, but nothing he'd said or done had.

"No," he said, and touched her arm. She flinched and tears welled up in her eyes.

"I couldn't pull the trigger. I just...couldn't."

"It's all right. We're all right. It's over."

She shook her head. "It was all so...senseless."

He knew that she came from an ordered life, one where things always added up and made sense. One and one were always two. She was shaken and remorseful and he would have done anything to change that. But just the sight of him was a reminder that she'd failed herself, and no matter what he said...

He recounted everything that had happened for the second time to the deputy marshal, and then signed the paper that was put in front of him. Lily was being questioned in a separate room. He could see her through the window. She was crying.

His heart ached and he wanted desperately to go to her. But when she happened to look up, her gaze met his and she quickly looked away.

As he left the room, he saw that Ace was waiting for his sister.

"You saved her," Ace said, and shook Tag's hand.

"It wasn't like that."

"Yeah, it was. You found her and got her out of there."

"I almost got her killed because of a stupid flash drive with useless names on it." Lily was right. It had all been for nothing. "Take good care of her."

"Where are you going?"

"Back to Texas. I'm the last person your sister wants to see right now."

Ace looked sad about that. Not half as sad as Tag. He told himself it would never have worked out anyway. He lived in Texas. She lived in Montana. Even if she wasn't going back to her ex... And yet he kept thinking of her hand against that dirty pane of glass and her face in the faint moonlight.

The ache was like a hard knot inside him. He and Lily had never stood a chance. That was all it had been. A chance encounter doomed from the start. So why did it feel as if he was losing something he would yearn for for the rest of his life?

As he looked out into the faint light of daybreak, he

heard Christmas music playing somewhere in the distance. Colorful lights glittered across the village of Big Sky. He hoped he could get the first flight out. He'd had all he could take of Christmas in Montana.

"You've been through a lot," Ace told Lily on the way back to his place. The sun was just starting to come up; the sky behind the mountains to the east was silvery with sunrise.

The day was cold and frosty, a misty fog hanging low in the snowcapped pines. Lily watched the landscape slide past and hugged herself even though it was warm in her brother's Jeep.

"I always thought I could take care of myself." She felt her brother glance over at her. "I've never thought of myself as helpless or weak."

"You are neither. I'm not sure I could have pulled that trigger, either."

She shot him a disappointed look. "We both know better than that."

"Come on, Lily. It's over. Cut yourself some slack. You were abducted. You could have been killed. You survived."

She nodded and looked out at the passing wild country. She'd survived but at what cost?

Ace reached over and squeezed her arm. "I'm so sorry. If I hadn't hired Mia in the first place—"

"You sound like Tag. He blames himself for finding the thumb drive when I was there. It's nobody's fault. It's just that it was all for nothing. The names were of no use. Everyone was killing each other for *nothing.* The list was of no use because half the names were wrong on it, I heard at the marshal's office. Apparently, Mia either messed up or they were onto her and gave her a fraudulent one."

Ace drove in silence the rest of the way to his apartment over the bar.

"I'm going to my own house," she said when she looked up and saw that her SUV was parked in the lot behind the bar.

He started to argue, but she cut him off. "All the bad guys are locked up. It's over. I want to go home. Need to go home."

"I don't like the idea of you being alone," her brother said.

She smiled at him. "I need to be alone. I'll drive down tomorrow. We can talk then. Right now—"

"I know, you just need to be alone," he finished for her, and smiled. "You've always been like that. I need people when I'm upset. You need solitude."

"Thank you for understanding."

"The marshal had your car picked up at Gerald's motel and brought here," he said. "Gerald stopped by earlier to say he was flying back to California. Does that mean you didn't take him back? You aren't reconsidering, are you?"

"Would that be so bad?" She held up a hand as her brother started to tell her again what he thought of Gerald. He didn't understand. Gerald offered her a quiet, safe life. Right now that sounded like just what she needed. She opened the passenger-side door of the Jeep and climbed out. "Tomorrow. We'll talk about it tomorrow."

With that she walked to her SUV, beeped open the driver's-side door and climbed in. She needed familiar right now, her own things around her. She turned the key in the ignition. The engine roared to life.

Her brother stood at the front door of the bar, waving as she left. She could tell he didn't like letting her go—letting her even consider going back to Gerald.

The past twenty-four hours were like a bad dream. Gerald showing up, making love with Tag, being kidnapped and held hostage and then Tag's rescue and, ultimately, her own part in it.

She could still remember the feel of the gun in her hand, the weight of it, the touch of the trigger. She'd let herself down. Let Tag down and almost gotten them both killed.

Her phone rang. She glanced at the caller ID. Tag. She couldn't bear to pick up. He would be flying home to his life in Texas. She'd heard him telling the deputy marshal of his plans.

"I need to go back to Houston," he'd said in response to the marshal's question about where he could be reached. "My brothers and I own a barbecue business."

"You're not staying for Christmas?"

Tag had glanced in her direction, and then said, "No, I don't think so."

He'd come over to her then and tried to talk to her, but she'd already put that cold, unemotional wall back up—the one Gerald had always admired about her. She could tell that Tag had been hurt and confused. He'd wanted to help her through this.

She shook her head at the thought as she pulled into her drive. There were tracks in the snow. But she didn't think too much about them. Everyone had been looking for her. Someone must have checked her house after the snow quit falling.

Lily pressed the garage-door opener and watched the door slowly rise in the cold mountain air before she pulled in. She'd just cut the engine, the door dropping behind her, and gotten out when she realized she wasn't alone.

As TAG WAS getting ready to leave the marshal's office, his father walked in. Tag wasn't up to seeing anyone right now, still stung from the rebuke Lily had given him. She'd acted the same way the morning after their lovemaking. In those moments earlier, she'd made it clear that there was nothing between the two of them.

So it wasn't surprising that he felt a lethal mixture of emotions at just the sight of Harlan Cardwell right then.

"Well, if it isn't my father the agent."

"Retired CIA agent," Harlan said.

"Whatever." He started to walk past him, but his father caught his arm. "We need to talk."

"Really? I flew all the way up here hoping that you might have five minutes for me. *Now* you want to talk? Let me guess. You want to talk about this case—not about you and me. You really don't know how to be a father, do you?"

"No, I don't," Harlan said. "I still need to talk to you."

Tag shook his head. He couldn't help the well of anger that boiled up in his belly. When he'd flown up here for Christmas, he'd told himself he'd had no expectations. That had been a lie. He'd come hoping to find the father he'd never had.

"Why don't we step into Hud's office?" his father said.

"Are you ordering me?"

"I'm asking."

They stood with their gazes locked for a few moments, before Tag relented and stepped into the office.

"Okay, let's get this debriefing over with," he said as Harlan closed the door behind them and motioned his son into one of the two chairs in front of Hud's desk.

"I'm sorry," his father said as he sat down. "You're right. I know nothing about being a father."

"And you never tried to learn."

"I did at first, but I let my job get in the way. It seemed more important."

Tag saw how hard that was for Harlan to admit. "It still is."

Harlan shook his head. "I only got involved because I used to work with Mia's father. I've known her since she was a baby. I could see that she was in over her head and yet…" He raked a hand through his hair. Tag noticed the streaks of gray he hadn't before. He saw the lines around his father's eyes. Saw how much he'd aged as if it had all been in the past twenty-four hours.

He'd seen his father as a guitar-playing, beer-drinking good ol' boy who just wanted to have fun. Now he saw the man behind that facade.

"Stay for Christmas," Harlan said.

"Was the computer thumb drive really worthless?" Tag asked. "Or is that just another lie?"

His father looked sad and disappointed for a moment that Tag had turned their conversation back to business, but finally said, "The original drive was corrupted."

Tag frowned. "Corrupted? Well, at least you have the list that Lily provided you."

"The names Lily McCabe decoded were incorrect. Useless, since there was no way to match up those ex-cons with the deaths of the law officers on the list."

Tag let out a curse. "Lily was so sure—"

"Some of them were right. I don't know why she

wasn't able to get the rest of them. But whatever the reason, it probably saved her life," Harlan said.

Tag felt his heart bump in his chest. He and Lily had tried so hard, but ultimately, they'd both failed. "So now what?"

"I'm retired again. That's why I'd like you to stay for Christmas."

A cheer came up from another part of the office. The dispatcher gave a thumbs-up and mouthed that Dana was going to make it.

"I'll think about it," Tag said, and rose to his feet. His father did the same and held out his hand. Tag shook it, feeling his father's strength in that big hand. "Did Mother know?"

Harlan nodded. "She couldn't live with never being sure if I was going to make it home for dinner."

Tag nodded.

"I hope you stay for Christmas, but I'll understand if you don't."

At the cabin, he packed up his things, realizing he couldn't leave without seeing Lily one more time and saying goodbye. He swung by the bar to find it closed. After a few minutes of pounding on the door, Ace appeared.

"Is Lily here?"

"She was determined to go to her place. I tried to talk her into staying with me, but my sister is one stubborn woman."

Tag smiled. "Determined and strong."

"Well, she's not feeling all that strong right now. She feels she let herself down and almost got you killed. I'm not sure she can ever forgive herself."

"It wasn't like that."

"Tell her that."

"I've tried."

Ace glanced toward the old pickup Tag was driving. "You're leaving."

"I am, but I don't want to go without seeing her again."

"She says she needs to be alone. Sorry."

"Okay." Tag turned to leave.

"I suppose you won't be back."

"Not likely," he said as he walked to his father's pickup and climbed in. The sun had come up behind the mountains and now washed the countryside with cold winter sunlight.

As he drove out of Big Sky, Tag found himself mentally kicking himself. If he hadn't gone to the bar that night and Mia hadn't stumbled into him... If he hadn't found that stupid thumb drive in his coat pocket and let Lily see it. If...

His heart began to pound as he remembered something. He turned around to head back toward Lone Mountain and called his father. "About those names. You said the thumb drive was corrupted and so was the copy Hud made, right? Lily told me that she had decoded some of them, but hadn't had a chance to finish. It was her former fiancé who gave us the list." Tag swore. "I let him use the original flash drive."

Harlan instantly was on alert. "What's his name?"

"Gerald Humphrey."

"What do you know about him?"

"Nothing. Nothing except that it took him six months to show up after he'd stood Lily up at the altar. He supposedly already left on a flight from Bozeman to Los Angeles, California, today."

He heard his father clicking on a computer keyboard. "I'm showing that he was on the flight."

"Is there any way to verify that?" Tag turned onto Lone Mountain Road and headed toward Lily's while he waited.

"I can try to contact the airport."

"But why would Gerald corrupt the thumb drive or give Lily the wrong names?" He could hear his father clacking away at the computer keyboard.

"He recently left his job in Montana to take a lesser one in California at a small private school," Harlan said. "Wait a minute. Next of kin. Gerald Humphrey has a younger sister who was recently sentenced for embezzlement. She got fifteen years and is serving time in a prison in California near the private school where he is now teaching."

Tag's mind raced. Was it possible Gerald was up to his neck in this? He hadn't come back to sweet-talk Lily into taking him back. He'd come back because Mia worked at the Canyon Bar—and she had managed to get the list. Tag cringed. He'd given the thumb drive to Gerald to decode and now it was corrupted.

"Lily mentioned something about Gerald taking a job in California," Tag said to his father. "This co-op killing group isn't just in Montana, is it? It's nationwide?"

"Tag—"

He floored the old pickup as he headed for Lily, praying he wasn't too late.

LILY FROZE AT the sight of a large dark figure standing in the doorway to the house. Her breath rushed from her as her heart took off on a downhill run.

"Lily, I knew you'd come alone."

"Gerald?" He moved then into the dim light so she could see his face. The familiarity of it let her suck in a

couple of calming breaths before she asked, "What are you doing here? I thought you flew back to California."

"I couldn't leave just yet," he said. "Are you going to just stand in the garage all day or come inside?"

She bristled at his tone, but quickly quelled her irritation. There was a reason Gerald treated her like a child. Around him she felt like one.

He was still blocking the door as she approached, but he moved aside at the last minute to let her into her own house. She glanced around. Everything looked just as it had yesterday before she'd left to meet him. Yesterday she'd been so sure of herself. So sure she wanted something different. *Someone* more exciting.

"I'm glad you didn't leave," she said as she took off her coat.

"Really?" Gerald took the coat and hung it up.

She noticed his was also on the coatrack by the front door—in the same place it had been just two nights before. He'd certainly made himself at home, she thought, noticing that he had a small fire going in her fireplace. She'd picked up the hint of smoke as she'd come in, but hadn't registered why until this moment.

Lily resisted the part of her that resented Gerald thinking he could just come in and do as he pleased in her house.

"How did you get into the house?" she asked suddenly, and glanced toward the front door, recalling locking it before she left.

"Through the garage. You do realize I am smarter than your garage-door opener, don't you?"

She studied him, faintly aware that he seemed different. That alone threw her since Gerald had always been so solidly…Gerald.

"I've never questioned how smart you are."

"Really?" he said as he moved around the dining room table, his thick fingers dragging along the smooth edge of the wood.

She saw him slow as he reached her computer and realized that all the paperwork she'd left on the table was gone. She shot a look toward the fire. One of the papers hadn't completely burned.

Her heart began to pound so hard she thought for sure he would hear it. She glanced toward the computer screen but couldn't read what was on it.

"I'm surprised that you never asked me why I decided to move to a small private school in California," Gerald said, drawing her attention back to him.

"I didn't really get a chance to ask before…" She let the rest of what she would have said yesterday die in her throat. She wasn't up to a fight with Gerald. His standing her up at the wedding no longer mattered. It seemed a lot more than six months ago.

"Yes, the wedding," he said, and stopped moving to look at her.

"I don't want to argue about—"

"I didn't come here to try to change your mind."

That surprised her. "Then I guess I don't understand."

"Don't you? I would have thought you of all people would have put it together by now. You were my best student. You disappoint me, Lily."

She frowned. "I don't know what you're talking about."

"The code."

With a sigh, her body heavy with exhaustion, weary from the events of the past twenty-four hours, she said, "None of that matters. The names were wrong anyway. I almost died for nothing. I almost got Tag—" She stopped herself.

"*Tag*. What kind of name is that anyway? Like Ace? Another name you might call your dog?"

Lily studied Gerald then, feeling the weight of the world settling on her shoulders, and said, "I'm sorry if I hurt you, Gerald. Is that what you need me to say? Is that what you're doing here? Because I just don't know what you want from me."

He took a step toward her. "There was a time you would have known." He shook his head as he stopped within inches of her and reached out to touch her cheek with his fingers.

She closed her eyes, trying not to think of Tag's touch, of Tag's embrace, of Tag.

"But that time has long passed."

She opened her eyes, hearing the thinly veiled anger in his voice. "That's why you missed your flight? You just wanted to tell me you don't love me anymore?" A stab of anger made her heart beat a little faster. "Fine. Give it your best shot. I've disappointed you. I'm not good enough for you. Whatever it is, let's hear it. Then leave." She had started to step past him when he grabbed her arm.

"You can't possibly think that I have gone to all this trouble just to have the last word. Don't you know me any better than that?" he demanded. "Are you so besotted with that cowboy that he's turned your brain to mush?"

She tried to jerk free of his hold, but he only tightened it. "So this is about jealousy? You didn't want me but you don't want anyone else to have me, either?"

"So he has had you." He swore, something she'd

never heard him do before. He'd always said that curs-ing was a lazy, uneducated waste of the vernacular.

She shot him a withering look.

"Stupid cow," Gerald snapped. "Didn't you even question once why your code and mine were so dif-ferent?"

Lily blinked, thrown off for a moment from the lightning-fast change of topic. "You said mine was off—"

"And you believed me." He laughed. "I guess I will always be the teacher and you will always be the pupil."

She stared at him as if seeing a stranger. She had wondered why she'd gotten some of the names right and yet others Gerald had said were wrong. If her original decoding had been accurate, then…

"I just assumed you were right and I was wrong," she said more to herself than to him. She saw how foolish that had been, not only with the code but also with her entire relationship with this man.

"Come on, my little pupil. *Think.* Don't you remem-ber me telling you about my younger sister who lives in California?" His fingers clutching her arm tightened painfully.

"You're hurting me, Gerald."

"I told you how proud I was of her, that she was even smarter than me," he said as if he hadn't heard her or was ignoring her. "Well, guess what? All that money she was making hand over fist? It was one big lie. Em-bezzlement. She used that magnificent brain of hers to steal, and worse, she got caught!"

"I don't understand what that—"

"They sent her to prison! *Prison!* They put her with common thieves and killers. My precious baby sister."

His throat worked, his last words coming out in a croak. Tears welled up in his eyes.

Her mind tried to make sense of what he was saying, but she was so emotionally and physically wrung out… She jerked free of his hold and took a step back, banging into the edge of the kitchen counter.

Looming over her, he glared at her as if she were the one who'd sent his sister to prison. "Do you know anything about prison, Lily? No, of course you wouldn't know what a woman like my sister has to do to survive there."

Lily felt a chill run the length of her spine. The murder list. Her mind leapt from that thought to the most obvious one. "You didn't come here after six months to try to get me back."

Gerald gave a laugh, but it came out sounding like a sob. *"Finally."* He met her gaze, his challenging. "I did what I had to do to keep my sister safe. Just as I am going to do what I have to now."

Lily gripped the kitchen counter behind her. She was so exhausted she was having trouble understanding what he was talking about. "Gerald, it doesn't matter anymore. They say the thumb drive was corrupted—"

"I destroyed the information on the thumb drive when your boyfriend let me use it to decode the names," he said with his usual arrogance. "The information is worthless. I also destroyed the paper copies you left at the motel. The one you left was worthless. The original is gone."

Her gaze went to her computer and he laughed.

"While I was waiting for you, I put a virus in your computer that by now has destroyed everything— including the hard drive. I figured you might have used your brother's computer at some point, so when I used it to give your boyfriend the names, I also made sure a virus will destroy all his data."

He was enjoying showing how superior he was to her and the rest of the world. She'd seen that trait in him but never quite like this. What scared her was the feeling that he'd come here to do more than gloat.

A bubble of fear rose in her throat until she thought she would choke on it. "So you took care of everything."

"Not quite," he said as he closed the narrow space between them. "There is only one more copy I need to destroy." He tapped her temple. "I used to be so jealous of the way you could remember the most random things. You could remember entire lists of numbers and letters." He smiled and nodded. "You do remember the original thumb drive lists, don't you? I knew it. You've never been able to hide anything from me."

Chapter Seventeen

Tag left the truck at the bottom of the last hill and ran the rest of the way up the road to Lily's house. He'd brought one of the guns from his father's hidden stash, but he was praying he wasn't going to have to use it.

Maybe Gerald really had gotten on the flight to California. Maybe the fact that he had a sister in prison had nothing to do with anything that had been going on.

Tag knew he was clutching at straws. There were two many coincidences. Gerald was up to his eyeballs in this. Worse, Tag had handed over the thumb drive to him. He'd trusted Gerald because he'd been so desperate to find Lily and get her out of this mess. He'd only gotten her in deeper.

Unfortunately there would be no way to prove Gerald had corrupted the thumb drive. Even the fact that he'd given the feds the wrong names could be swept under the rug as a simple mistake.

So why would Gerald do anything stupid right now when he could walk away free?

Because Lily still had a copy of the information on her computer, Tag thought with a sinking heart.

As he neared the house, he prayed he would find Lily alone, Gerald long gone.

But when he climbed up onto the deck and moved to

the front window, he saw Lily and Gerald in the kitchen. He didn't need to hear what they were saying to each other. He could tell by their body language and their expressions that they were arguing.

His stomach roiled at the sight. Lily was backed up against the kitchen counter. Gerald was looming over her.

Tag tried the door, not surprised to find it locked. He was afraid to knock. He needed the element of surprise, and even with it he feared what would happen next.

He picked up a large flowerpot from the deck and, stepping back, hurled it through the window. Glass rained down in a shower onto the deck as the huge window shattered.

Pulling his gun, Tag quickly jumped through the opening into Lily's living room.

Gerald had turned in surprise at the sound of the breaking glass. His eyes widened at the gun in Tag's hands.

"Get away from him!" Tag yelled as he strode toward them, the gun aimed at Gerald's chest.

Lily seemed nailed to the floor. Her eyes widened in alarm, her mouth opened as if to scream, but nothing came out.

In that instant, Gerald took advantage of her inability to move and grabbed her, locking his arm around her throat as he backed the two of them against the kitchen counter.

"That's far enough," Gerald said as Tag advanced. "Come any closer and I'll break her neck."

Tag stopped at the edge of the dining room. Out of the corner of his eye, he saw Lily's laptop still open on the table, but the papers she'd been doing her decoding on were gone and there was the faint smell of smoke from the fireplace in the room.

"Drop your gun. Slowly," Gerald ordered.

Tag could see the painful hold Gerald had on Lily and knew he couldn't get a shot off without risking her life. Gerald was using her like a shield. Tag slowly lowered his gun, but didn't drop it.

"What's going on, Gerald?" he asked as he carefully bent down and placed his weapon on the floor, never taking his eyes off Lily's.

"Now kick the gun over here."

Tag did as he was told. The gun skittered across the floor. Gerald slowly reached down, dragging Lily with him, and picked up the gun with his free hand, never releasing his hold on her.

"You really should have gone back to Texas and left Lily alone."

LILY HAD FELT too tired to fight Gerald earlier. Now things had changed. She found a reserved strength she hadn't known she possessed. Gerald had the gun pointed at Tag. For the second time in two days, she was faced with a life-or-death situation after more than thirty-two years of an ordered, overly structured life. The only time she'd felt she wasn't in control was when she came up here to the Canyon to work for her brother.

Until this.

"Let him go," Lily said hoarsely from the choke hold on her throat. "This is between you and me."

Gerald's laugh held no humor. "That might have been the case yesterday when I pleaded with you to come back to me. Maybe we could have worked something out then…."

"You sold out your own fiancée," Tag said as he took

a step toward the dining room, forcing Gerald to turn a little in order to keep her in front of him.

"Ex-fiancée," Gerald snapped, and motioned the gun at him. "Didn't she mention that to you? I'm surprised. I thought the two of you…"

"That's what I planned to tell you," Lily said. She shifted so she was closer to the kitchen counter. Her hand snaked behind her as she sought out the drawer where she'd dropped the gun earlier. "I was hoping it wasn't too late for us, Gerald. I wanted the life you offered where I knew who I was." There was a ring of truth to her words since that was exactly what she'd been thinking on her way home.

Tag's gaze widened a little, his expression saddening.

"It's not too late, Gerald," she continued as she eased the drawer open. "As you said, there's no proof you've done anything wrong. You've destroyed everything, all that you need to worry about anyway. If you kill this man, then that all changes."

She eased the drawer open, feeling Gerald loosen the hold on her a little. Her fingers curled around the handle of the gun.

"You had second thoughts?" Gerald said quietly next to her ear.

She nodded. His hold loosened even a little more. She could breathe, and for a moment that was all she did. Then she slowly lifted out the gun, holding it at her side out of his range of sight. "I was going to come back to you."

As if he felt the truth in her words, his surprise moved through his body. He seemed to slump against her.

"I don't understand," he whispered.

Tag was looking at her as if he didn't understand, either.

"I wanted safe," she said.

"Safe?" Gerald repeated, and let out a hoarse laugh, the irony not lost on him.

Tag's gaze went to her side. He gave a small shake of his head at the sight of the gun clutched in her hand.

"Nothing has changed," Gerald said, his tone almost pleading. "We can get past this. Our lives can be exactly like we planned. Even better after this."

Lily had to bite her tongue. Did he really think they could pick up where they'd left off? All forgiven and forgotten?

He was crazier than she'd thought.

In the distance, she heard sirens and realized how badly this could go if she didn't move quickly. "Tag, you should go," she said.

Gerald shook his head and tightened his hold on her. "Lily. We can't let him just walk away. Not now."

"We have to, Gerald. It's the only way."

But even as she said it, she felt Gerald tense the arm holding the gun. He leveled it at Tag's heart. "I'm sorry, Lily, but I think it's too late for us."

TAG KNEW WHEN he came through the door that Gerald was dangerous. The man had come too far and knew there was no turning back. Gerald Humphrey had crossed a line that a man like him couldn't come back from.

For just an instant, Tag felt sorry for him. He could understand wanting to protect someone you loved.

He looked down the barrel of the gun Gerald had pointed at him, saw the man steady it and knew all the talking was done.

At the same time, Tag saw Lily make the decision.

"No!" he yelled as he dived to the side. The first gunshot was followed only an instant later by a second.

The scream that filled the air made the hair rise on the back of his neck. He hit the floor and rolled, coming up to find Gerald Humphrey on the floor holding the thigh of his right leg and writhing in pain.

Lily stood over him, the gun still in her hand, her face as white as the snow outside. Gerald had gotten off one shot before dropping his weapon and grabbing his wounded leg.

Tag quickly stepped to him to kick his gun away before reaching to take the pistol from Lily. She had a death grip on the gun. He eased it from her fingers.

She gave him a barely perceptible nod.

He smiled as he cupped a hand behind her neck and drew her to him, wrapping her in his arms. She hugged him tightly as he breathed the words into the soft, sweet scent of her hair. "You saved my life."

On the floor, Gerald began to curse. "Are the two of you just going to let me lie here and bleed to death? Call a doctor!"

In the distance, Tag could hear the sirens. He pulled out his cell phone, hit 911 and asked for an ambulance as flashing lights flickered across the fallen snow outside the window. Tag watched his father and Deputy Marshal Jake Thorton come racing up to the house, weapons drawn, and pulled Lily closer.

Chapter Eighteen

Christmas Eve it began to snow and became one of those winter nights when the flakes are as large as goose feathers. They drifted down in a wall of white so thick they obliterated everything out the window at Cardwell Ranch.

"Merry Christmas," Tag said as he came up behind Lily.

She leaned back into him and watched the falling snow to the sound of Christmas music and children's laughter. In the kitchen, Stacy and the kids were finishing up baking gingerbread men. Dana had been relegated to sitting at the kitchen table and helping ice the cookies. The smell of ginger wafted through the old ranch house, mingling with the even sweeter scent of evergreen.

Lily could hear her brother in the kitchen. He'd volunteered to help with the cookie decorating, as well. She'd never seen Ace with kids before. He was a natural.

"I always dreamed of a Christmas like this," Lily said, turning in Tag's arms to look up into his face. "I would come home from boarding school to find the house was already decorated by some designer my mother had hired. We always had a white-flocked tree with different-colored lights on it depending on what was in that year. Everything was very…tasteful."

"Compared to an amazing tree like this one?" Tag joked, nodding toward Dana's "orphan" tree.

Lily laughed. The tree wasn't what most would consider a Christmas tree, but she loved that it was decorated with ornaments the children had made. Her mother would never have allowed a tree like that in her house.

How different her life and Ace's would have been if her mother had adopted an orphan tree and let her children decorate it. Would Lily have ever agreed to marry a man like Gerald Humphrey?

She thought of Gerald. He'd confessed to everything but refused to name names to protect himself in prison—as well as his sister. Lily had been able to supply the letters from the original thumb drive from memory. After they were decoded, the FBI had the names and was now rounding up the former inmates who had done the killings. For the time being at least, the co-op murder group had been shut down.

"That is the most beautiful Christmas tree I have ever seen," she said, feeling tears sting her eyes as she turned to look at him. They'd been through so much together in such a short time and yet she felt as if she had always known him.

Tag cocked an eyebrow at her, then smiled and pulled her in for a kiss.

"You're only supposed to kiss under the misseytoe," said a small voice behind them. Lily turned to find Dana's daughter, Mary, pointing at the mistletoe hanging near the door. "That's where Mommy and Daddy kiss."

Mary's older brother, Hank, came into the room in

time to make a grimacing face. "They are always kissing. Gross."

Tag and Lily laughed. A moment later Ace came into the room carrying a tray of gingerbread men. The twins, Angus and Brick, now fourteen months old and their cousin, Ella, now almost two, came toddling into the room following the cookies. They had icing smeared across their faces. They were followed by their aunt Stacy with a washcloth.

"I decorated those," Ace said with obvious pride as he pointed to the perfectly decorated cookies.

"I did those," Mary said, pointing to some cookies that were unrecognizable under all the different colors of icing.

"I can't tell the difference." Lily grinned at her brother.

Hud and Dana joined them, Dana in the wheelchair her husband had insisted she stay in until she was stronger. She was plenty strong, Lily thought. She recalled her own moments over the past few days when she'd been stronger than she'd ever believed she could be. So much had changed, she thought, glancing over at Tag. Or maybe she'd just changed. She would never admit it to her brother, but she had been afraid to live life. She'd thought she'd wanted safe and sedate, just as she and Ace had been raised.

But Tag had changed all that. No matter what happened in the future, she knew she could never go back to being the woman who'd been willing to settle for what Gerald Humphrey had offered her.

AT THE SOUND of sleigh bells, everyone in the room went quiet. Christmas music played faintly from the kitchen as heavy boots stomped across the porch. An instant later the door flew open and a Santa Claus suspiciously resembling Tag's father filled the doorway.

Mary and Hank let out cheers and ran to him. Santa was followed into the house by Angus dragging a huge bag loaded with gifts. Tag looked at Lily and saw the delight in her face. He wished he could see that look on her face always.

Jordan and his very pregnant wife, Deputy Marshal Liza Cardwell, arrived moments later with presents. Not long after that, Dana's brother, Clay, landed by helicopter out by the barn in a shower of snow. He came in signing Christmas carols and got them all singing around the fireplace and the orphan tree.

As Tag felt Harlan's aka Santa's arm drop over his shoulders, a lump formed in his throat. He'd wanted a Montana Christmas, and he couldn't have asked for a more perfect one than this.

He wished this night would never end, he thought as he watched his family opening presents around the tree. But the holidays were almost over and Texas and the rest of his family and their business loomed large on the horizon.

LILY WOKE JUST as the sun was peeking over the mountains. She hadn't wanted to open her eyes. Lying under the down comforter, she was warm and cozy, still feeling the effects of her lovemaking with Tag not that many hours ago.

It had been the best Christmas Eve of her life and she thought it funny she could think that, given that she'd almost been killed in the days before. Last night, Tag had been so gentle. She shivered at the thought. He'd brought her back to her house after midnight, swept her up into his arms and carried her to the bed.

He'd kissed her so gently, so sweetly. She'd thought she'd only imagined the passion from their first love-making. But then the kisses had become more amorous. She'd felt heat race through her veins, making her skin sensitive to the touch. He'd peeled away her clothing, kissing each patch of skin he revealed, finding places on her body to caress as if memorizing every inch of her.

She'd reciprocated, loving the feel of his skin and the way he shuddered with delight as she moved over him. They kissed and touched until, both naked and barely able to contain themselves, they'd finally coupled. Locked in each other's arms, they'd let their passion run wild like the storm outside.

Just the thought of their lovemaking made Lily reach over to the other side of her bed, expecting to find Tag's warm body. Earlier they'd been spooned together.

Her eyes flew open. The bed was empty. Loss raced through her on the heels of fear. Would Tag just leave? Last night he'd said he didn't know how he would be able to tell her goodbye when the holidays were over. Had he gone back to Texas?

Grabbing her silk robe, she moved toward the living room, terrified she would find a scribbled note and Tag Cardwell gone.

But as she rounded the corner, she did a double take. With everything that had been going on, she hadn't had time to do the little decorating she normally did for Christmas.

That was why she was shocked to see a large beautiful Christmas tree standing in the front window. It shone with an array of colored lights and ornaments. Tag stood in front of it wearing nothing but a pair of jeans.

She looked at him in surprise.

He grinned. "You like it? I got Hank and Mary to

make ornaments for it, and my father gave me some of the ones from when I was a child."

Tears welled up in her eyes. "I *love* it."

"I wanted you to have that old-fashioned Christmas you always dreamed of—not just the one at Cardwell Ranch."

She rushed to him and threw her arms around his neck. "Oh, Tag."

He held her to him, the lights of the tree flickering in the early-morning light. "I can't leave you, Lily. And I can't ask you to quit your job to move to Texas," he said finally, holding her at arm's length.

She tried to swallow past the lump in her throat.

TAG LOOKED INTO Lily's beautiful face and felt so much love for her that it nearly knocked him to his knees.

"There is only one thing I can do," he said. "It was actually my father's idea."

Last night, Harlan had stopped him as Tag and Lily were leaving Cardwell Ranch. "Are you really headed back to Texas?"

"Christmas is over," Tag had said as Lily walked on out to her SUV they had arrived in. "I have a business to run with my brothers."

"I just wish we'd had some time to get to know each other better."

Tag had laughed at that. "Oh, I think we got to know each other quite well."

"I'm serious. I wish you would stay longer. You know Big Sky could really use a good Texas barbecue joint."

"Your father gave you the idea?" Lily said now.

He nodded, smiling. "He thinks I should open a Texas Boys Barbecue joint in Big Sky. What do you think?"

She laughed and leaned up to kiss him. "That is the best Christmas present I could have asked for."

"Really?" he asked with a grin. "Then I guess I'll have to take this back." He drew a small dark velvet box out of his pocket. "I was going to wait until later under the Christmas tree, but I can't wait another moment."

Her heart began to pound.

"I know it probably seems fast—"

She shook her head and he laughed.

"Yeah, that's kind of the way I feel," he said, and he opened the box. The winter light caught the diamond, sending a prism of brilliant light ricocheting around the room.

"I love you, Lily McCabe. Marry me someday? Someday soon?"

Lily laughed and nodded through her tears as he slipped the ring on her finger.

* * * * *

REQUEST YOUR FREE BOOKS!
2 FREE NOVELS PLUS 2 FREE GIFTS!

H HARLEQUIN®

INTRIGUE®

BREATHTAKING ROMANTIC SUSPENSE

YES! Please send me 2 FREE Harlequin Intrigue® novels and my 2 FREE gifts (gifts are worth about $10). After receiving them, if I don't wish to receive any more books, I can return the shipping statement marked "cancel." If I don't cancel, I will receive 6 brand-new novels every month and be billed just $4.74 per book in the U.S. or $5.24 per book in Canada. That's a savings of at least 14% off the cover price! It's quite a bargain! Shipping and handling is just 50¢ per book in the U.S. and 75¢ per book in Canada.* I understand that accepting the 2 free books and gifts places me under no obligation to buy anything. I can always return a shipment and cancel at any time. Even if I never buy another book, the two free books and gifts are mine to keep forever.

182/382 HDN F42N

Name _____ (PLEASE PRINT) _____

Address _____ Apt. #

City _____ State/Prov. _____ Zip/Postal Code

Signature (if under 18, a parent or guardian must sign)

Mail to the **Harlequin® Reader Service:**
IN U.S.A.: P.O. Box 1867, Buffalo, NY 14240-1867
IN CANADA: P.O. Box 609, Fort Erie, Ontario L2A 5X3
Are you a subscriber to Harlequin Intrigue books
and want to receive the larger-print edition?
Call 1-800-873-8635 or visit www.ReaderService.com.

* Terms and prices subject to change without notice. Prices do not include applicable taxes. Sales tax applicable in N.Y. Canadian residents will be charged applicable taxes. Offer not valid in Quebec. This offer is limited to one order per household. Not valid for current subscribers to Harlequin Intrigue books. All orders subject to credit approval. Credit or debit balances in a customer's account(s) may be offset by any other outstanding balance owed by or to the customer. Please allow 4 to 6 weeks for delivery. Offer available while quantities last.

Your Privacy—The Harlequin® Reader Service is committed to protecting your privacy. Our Privacy Policy is available online at www.ReaderService.com or upon request from the Harlequin Reader Service.

We make a portion of our mailing list available to reputable third parties that offer products we believe may interest you. If you prefer that we not exchange your name with third parties, or if you wish to clarify or modify your communication preferences, please visit us at www.ReaderService.com/consumerschoice or write to us at Harlequin Reader Service Preference Service, P.O. Box 9062, Buffalo, NY 14269. Include your complete name and address.

HI13R

*Her target is tall, dark and dangerous…but now a vengeful
enemy is targeting them both. As the enemy lurks closer,
Eden Gray and federal marshal Declan O'Malley must fight
for a future they might not live to see.*

"I've watched you for the past two days, so I knew you take a
ride this time of morning before you go into work."

"You watched me?"

She nodded.

"Are you going to make me arrest you, or do you plan to keep
going with that explanation?"

"I'm a P.I. now. I own a small agency in San Antonio."

She'd skipped right over the most important detail of her
brief bio. "Your father's Zander Gray, a lowlife, swindling scum.
I arrested him about three years ago for attempting to murder a
witness who was going to testify against him, and he was doing
hard time before he escaped."

And this was suddenly becoming a whole lot clearer.

"He sent you here," Declan accused.

"No," she quickly answered. "But my father might have been
the reason they contacted me in the first place," Eden explained.
"They might have thought I'd do anything to get back at you for
arresting him. I won't."

He made a sound of disagreement. "Since you're trespassing

and have been stalking me, convince me otherwise that you're not here to avenge your father."

"I'm not." Not a whisper that time. And there was some fire in those two little words. "But someone's trying to set me up."

Declan thought about that a second. "Lady, if you wanted me to investigate that, you didn't have to follow me or come to my ranch. My office is on Main Street in town."

Another head shake. "They didn't hire me to go to your office."

"So, who are they?"

"I honestly don't know." She dodged his gaze, tried to turn away, but he took hold of her again to force her to face him. "After I realized someone had planted that false info on my computer, I got a call from a man using a prepaid cell phone. I didn't recognize his voice. He said if I went to the cops or the marshals, he'd release the info on my computer, that I'd be arrested."

"This unknown male caller is the one who put the camera outside?"

"I think so."

He shook his head. "If they sent you to watch me, why use a camera?"

"Because the camera is to watch *me*," she clarified. "To make sure I do what he ordered me to do."

"And what exactly are you supposed to do?" Declan demanded.

Eden Gray shoved her hand over her Glock. "I'm to kill you."

Will Eden and Declan be able to work together, or will their past get in the way?

Don't miss the edge-of-your-seat action in
JUSTICE IS COMING
by USA TODAY bestselling author Delores Fossen.
Available November 19, only from Harlequin Intrigue.

HARLEQUIN®

INTRIGUE®

THREATS INSTEAD OF CHRISTMAS CARDS

As the lone surviving victim who can put her attacker away in prison, heiress Bailey Austin becomes the key to the D.A.'s case against a notorious criminal. As lead detective, Spencer Montgomery must prep her for trial. But he becomes her personal protector when she starts receiving terrifying "gifts" meant to scare her away from testifying. Her courage touches him in ways no other woman has, and reminds him that she's more important to him than any investigation.

YULETIDE PROTECTOR

BY *USA TODAY* BESTSELLING AUTHOR

JULIE MILLER

Available November 19, only from Harlequin® Intrigue®.

HI69729

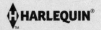

INTRIGUE

THE OLD SAYING IS TRUE:
THE SMALLER THE TOWN,
THE BIGGER THE SECRETS

People in town believe Tawny-Lynn Boulder is the reason
the Camden Cross case went unsolved. She survived
the bus accident that left several dead and two missing,
but the severe trauma left her with amnesia. When she
returns seven years later, Sheriff Chaz Camden reopens
the case and asks for her help. But someone in town
keeps threatening to kill Tawny-Lynn to keep the case
closed. Now she must trust the sexy sheriff for protection.
Together, they'll show this murderer that in Camden,
accidents don't happen…justice does.

COLD CASE AT
CAMDEN CROSSING
BY RITA HERRON

Available November 19, only from Harlequin® Intrigue®.